BLOOD OF THE HORSETOOTH WIDOW

A Yakima Henry Western

PETER BRANDVOLD

WOLFPACK
PUBLISHING
— EST 2013 —

Published in the United States by Wolfpack Publishing,
Las Vegas

Wolfpack Publishing
5130 S. Fort Apache Road, 215-380
Las Vegas, NV 89148

wolfpackpublishing.com

Paperback ISBN 978-1-64734-618-8
eBook ISBN 978-1-64734-617-1

BLOOD OF THE
HORSETOOTH WIDOW

1

The red-bearded bartender swung his freckled face toward the tall, dark man in a calico shirt and smoke-stained buckskin trousers just then pushing through the batwings of the Horsetooth Saloon & Hotel, and said, "Pardon me all to hell, breed, but you'd best take two steps back the way you came and read the sign posted to the front wall there!"

Yakima Henry stared at the bartender. The man stared back at him, frowning belligerently, a cleaver in one hand, a chunk of bloody rabbit in the other. There were a half dozen other men in the dim, dingy place—three at a table near the front of the room, two more at a table near the bar, two more near the cold, potbelly stove. No fire was needed. The dry desert air was hot and oppressive, mixing the smells of the pent up saloon—raw meat, hot bodies, coal oil, tobacco, and cheap liquor—until it smelled like a bear den. The three at the near table, all hard-bitten, pie-eyed men in cheap suits ensconced in billowing clouds of cigarette smoke, stared at Yakima with expressions that were a nasty hybrid of distaste and cruel delight.

A dog had just sauntered into their camp. They didn't like dogs.

"You hear me, breed?" the barman said. "Step back out there and read the cotton-pickin' sign. I put it up there for a *reason!*"

Yakima gave a sheepish smile. "I reckon you're gonna have to come on out and read it for me, mister."

The barman chuckled. "Can't read, huh?"

The three men in cheap suits, which marked them as salesmen of a sort, laughed and snickered though Yakima doubted they could read half as well as he'd taught himself to from whatever books he'd been able to get his hands on over his long years on the remote western frontier.

He doubted the bar tender could read as well as he could, either.

The barman sighed with strained tolerance, plopped the meat chunk into the pot, and set the cleaver down on the bar. As he walked out from behind the counter, he wiped his hands on his apron though Yakima doubted anyone could actually clean his hands on such a badly stained scrap of tattered cloth.

The barman was several inches short of six feet, but

he was built like two rain barrel-sized slabs of suet sitting one atop the other. He smelled like sweat, raw meat, and whiskey. As he stepped out from behind the bar, he gave his hands another scrub on the apron and strode past Yakima and out the batwings, holding the left wing open as he pointed.

"There it is right there. Come on out here—I'll give you a little lesson in English."

He beckoned to Yakima. The half-breed shrugged, stepped halfway through the batwings, and followed the man's pale, pudgy finger to the sign nailed to the front wall right of the doors. It was a rough pine board on which someone had hand-painted blocky letters in dark-green trimmed liberally with dried drips.

The portly barman pointed out each word in turn as he read, "If yur skin is any darker than these dors"—he paused and slapped the top of the sun-bleached batwing he was holding open—"then you can kiss my ass and point your hat in the oppositt direction!"

The men inside the saloon laughed.

The barman opened his mouth to show his teeth and then he laughed, as well, thoroughly delighted with himself.

"Give me your hand," he told Yakima, as though he were speaking to a moron.

Yakima glanced at the other customers, gave another

sheepish hike of his right shoulder, and then gave the man his right hand.

"That's it—there you go. You're catchin' on." The barman held Yakima's hand, which was nearly the color of an old penny—heavily callused, scarred, and weathered—up beside the batwing door.

The bartender clucked and shook his head as though the contrast saddened him. "No, no. Now, you see there—that skin of yours is about seven, eight shades darker than these here doors. That means you're about as welcome on these premises as a goddamn full-blood Apache. Why, you're no more welcome here than Geronimo himself. You see?"

He grinned at Yakima, who stood a whole half a head taller. Yakima stared down at the fat man from beneath the flat brim of his low-crowned, broad-brimmed, black Stetson.

Yakima pulled his hand from the bar tender's grip and used it to indicate the words painted on the pine board. "The sign says I should 'kiss-your-ass', right?"

The man's smile faltered and a slight flush pinkened the nubs of his fat, freckled cheeks. "Say again?"

"The sign there says that if my skin is any darker than these doors, I should kiss your ass."

The barman gave a nervous chuckle, snorted, and glanced at the sign. "Well, now, that it does, that it does."

The men inside had fallen silent. They were all holding their drinks and cigarettes or cigars in their hands and staring with bright-eyed interest at the doings at the doors.

"Well, then," Yakima said. "Let's step inside so I can do the honors."

"What's that?"

"I said, let's go inside so I can kiss your ass like the sign says."

The barman stared up at him, but now his smile looked glued on and his cheeks were growing pinker. The men inside were snickering, one lightly slapping the back of his hand against his partner's shoulder. Yakima held the barman's gaze with a stony one of his own.

"What're you talkin' about?" the barman said.

"Isn't that what the sign says?"

From inside, one of the card players said, "Come on in, Clancy. If the breed wants to kiss your ass, let him kiss your ass. We'll watch to make sure he does it proper."

The barman stared up at Yakima, his smile fading fast though the flush was still building in his cheeks, darkening his freckles. He rolled his eyes around, and then sucked his lower lip and pooched out his cheeks and gave a fake laugh, as though the joke were still on the half-breed, and said, "Well, hell, yeah! That is what the sign says, all right!"

He laughed and walked inside the saloon and stopped and faced the bar. "Okay, there you go, Injun. Pucker up now!"

He looked at the card players and the two men sitting closer to the bar—one of the two was dressed in a dusty blue cavalry uniform. They and the drummers were all watching with keen interest now. The barman winked at the grinning, blond soldier, and snorted another nervous laugh.

"I want a nice soft one there on my left cheek." He leaned forward and patted his ass.

"Best drop your trousers," Yakima said, standing in front of the batwings, thumbs hooked behind his two cartridge belts. "So I can do it proper."

"Go ahead, Clancy," one of the card players said, laughing with the others. "Drop your pants so the breed can kiss your ass proper!"

He whooped as the others laughed and yelled.

"Go ahead, Clancy," said the beefy gent in common trail garb, sitting with the soldier, drinking beer.

"Pull 'em down, Clancy—what're you waiting for?" said the soldier.

"Oh, this is plush," said one of the others. "This is pure-dee plush! Pull 'em down, Clancy. Give him your fat, white ass so's he can lay a kiss on it!"

Clancy looked over his shoulder at Yakima. His grin

looked as though it had been chiseled in granite. "That's all right. You can just kiss my pants. Don't want them half-breed lips touchin' my delicate skin. I'll likely catch somethin' the local sawbones can't cure!"

"Oh, come on, Clancy!" yelled one of the card players farther back in the room. "Drop your pants. Show the breed what a fat white ass looks like!"

"Yeah, come on, Clancy!"

The others whooped and hollered. One slapped the table with both hands. One of the card players stuck his two little fingers in his mouth and whistled.

The fat man turned around and glared up at Yakima. He said only loudly enough for Yakima to hear beneath the din, "What do you think you're doin'?"

"I'm gonna kiss your ass—like the sign says."

"What—you a pervert or somethin'?"

"I didn't make the sign."

The barman curled his upper lip at the half-breed and then shaped a grin as he turned toward the others in the room, throwing up his arms and saying, "All right, all right! The Injun wants to kiss my ass, who'm I to refuse? Shit, it's on the sign, ain't it?" He glanced at Yakima. "Then you can haul your ass out of here!"

"You tell him, Clancy!" yelled the beefy gent at the near table.

Chuckling nervously, the bar tender walked over to

the bar, removed his apron, and tossed it onto the bar. He slipped his suspenders down his arms, unbuckled his baggy, blood stained canvas pants, and let them drop down around his ankles. He wore no other shirt than his longhandle top. He unbuttoned the top and slid it down his arms and down his legs.

The others in the room had fallen quiet. They were like a crowd in an opera house when the curtain rises. A couple rose to get a better look. The others snickered as they shifted around in their chairs.

Laughing loudly, jeeringly, the barman leaned forward against the bar, slapped his right butt cheek, making the pale, hairy flesh quiver, and yelled, "You wanna kiss my ass, breed? Well, there ya go—pucker up and kiss away!"

Yakima thrust his left hand against the back of the man's stout neck, holding his head fast against the bar top. With his other hand, he slid his horn-handled Colt .44 from the holster positioned for the cross-draw on his left hip, and clicked the hammer back.

"Hey, wha...what the hell you doin'?" the barman said, struggling against Yakima's iron grip. "Hey, now... *oh-eeeee-heeee!*"

The others in the room fell deathly quiet as the half-breed rammed the barrel of his cocked Colt against the barman's pink asshole. The man tried to lift his head but Yakima kept it pressed taut to the bar.

Yakima twisted the Colt a little and said in a low, menacing voice, "There you go, you fat son of a bitch—I'm kissin' your ass. How do you like it?"

The barman grunted and groaned, struggling against the half-breed's grip. Yakima shoved the barrel a little farther into the hole, and turned it, raking the rim of the barman's anus with the revolver's front site. The barman lifted his head and loosed a high wail.

None of the other men were saying anything. Aside from the barman's wailing, the room was as silent as a boneyard at midnight.

"You had enough of my kissin' your ass?" Yakima asked the barman, twisting his pistol barrel in the other direction.

"Yes!"

"Invite my to sit down and have a drink."

"Huh?"

"Invite me to sit down and have a drink, and you'd better be real polite about it, because—you know what? I find I kinda like kissin' this big, fat, white, ugly, smelly ass of yours!"

"Sit down and have a drink!" the barman wailed.

"On the house?"

"On the house! Oh, for chrissakes, I'll give you a whole fuckin' bottle! Whatever you like!"

Yakima pulled his pistol barrel out of the man's ass and

wiped it with a bar rag. "That's right friendly of you, pard. Don't mind if I do. I'll take a bottle of tequila. A fresh one."

The barman was panting as though he'd run a long ways, his lungs raking like a smithy's bellows. He scowled at Yakima as he turned around to lean back against the bar, and then he wrinkled his nose at the laughing customers.

He leaned forward, pulled his longhandles and his canvas trousers up his thick, pasty legs, and looped his suspenders over his shoulders. He walked a little stiffly, wincing, sweat dribbling down his freckled cheeks, around behind the bar and set a clear bottle onto the planks. He set a shot glass down beside the bottle. He glowered at Yakima over the bottle.

"Thanks, pard," Yakima said. "'Preciate it."

"Don't mention it."

Yakima took the bottle and the shot glass and moved through the tables of grinning, snickering men, to a vacant table along the saloon's far, adobe-brick wall, under an unlit bracket lamp. Rage still burned in him. This wasn't the first time he'd been harassed for the russet tones of his skin. He was part-Cheyenne, part Yakima, and part-German though aside from his jade-green eyes he looked more Indian than northern European.

Still, the prejudice chafed him. When he was riled, there was usually trouble, for he was bigger than most men. And he knew how to fight. He was pushing thirty after a long and varied career on the western frontier, but he still had not yet learned to turn the other cheek.

He doffed his broad-brimmed, low-crowned, black hat, ran a big, red paw through his long, coal-black hair that was still sweaty and dusty from the trail. He'd just come through the White Mountains headed for the border. Why, he didn't know. Mexico would be as good a place as any to look for work to see him and his horse, Wolf, through another couple of months.

It would be winter up north soon, and he liked to stay as far away from snow as possible. He'd had enough of snow. And of trouble up north, for that matter . . .

He grabbed the bottle. He shouldn't drink the tequila. The Mexican firewater, probably mostly mescal, would likely only add kerosene to the already hotly burning blaze inside him. He knew that from experience.

What the hell.

He popped the cork, splashed the colorless liquid into the shot glass, and tossed back the entire shot at once.

"Hey, Clancy, how's your ass feel after the half-breed's kiss?" asked one of the drummers. He was red-faced drunk as were the two other drummers sitting at his table. "Me an' the boys're thinkin' you rather liked it!"

Laughter all around.

Yakima splashed another round of tequila into his

shot glass. Out the corner of his left eye, he saw the barman turn away from the range on which he'd set the stew pot. The man's face was crimson, his little pig eyes bright with rage, his long, stringy hair hanging down against his suety cheeks.

"Yeah, really?" he barked, reaching under his plank bar that was as rough-hewn and humble as everything else in the earthen floored, smoky, smelly place. "Well, why don't I just show you how much I liked it!"

Yakima turned to see the man haul up a big, double-barreled shotgun from beneath the bar. The man had just ratcheted both heavy hammers back when, moving instinctively and automatically, Yakima whipped up his Peacemaker from his cross-draw holster, extended the Colt quickly but adeptly straight out from his right shoulder, and drilled a hole through the barman's forehead.

The slug threw the portly bastard straight back against his cook stove, sending the stew pot to the floor.

The barman didn't make a sound as he slid down the front of the hot stove, the smell of scorched flesh instantly filling the room, for he was already shaking hands with the red-eyed, yellow-toothed demons in Hell long before he hit the floor.

16

2

"What in the hell is that racket!" a woman's voice careened into the main drinking hall from the dilapidated saloon/hotel's second story. The voice was Spanish-accented. Yakima heard a light, feminine tread, and then the woman was leaning over the balcony rail, glaring down into the bar. "What is that shooting about?"

"The breed here shot your husband, Miss Paloma!" one of the drummers yelled, pointing an accusing finger toward Yakima. "That one there. He shot ole Clancy!"

Ah Christ, Yakima thought, his gut tightening.

The woman stared over the balcony rail into the area behind the bar where her husband lay dead. Yakima stared at her, waiting. He was surprised when she did not scream or sob or show any emotion at all but only slowly turned her head with its long, tresses of thick, wavy hair so dark that it owned a bluish sheen, and regarded the half-breed with pursed lips.

Yakima's gut tightened again, for the woman he was staring at was spectacularly beautiful. At least, she appeared spectacular from this distance.

He couldn't see all of the details of her face, but it definitely appeared superb, and there was no doubting the richness of her body clad in a metallic green and gold floral print dress that hugged her narrow waist and pushed up her ample bust that was only partly concealed by a fringe of white lace. Silver hoops dangled from her ears. Her arms beneath the dress's three or four-inch sleeves were pale and fine, her hands long-fingered and feminine, with silver rings on both her middle fingers.

She was one well set-up creature. About as well proportioned as a man could find. No doubt about it. So well-made, in fact, that Yakima felt chagrined at the warm stirrings in his loins so close on the heels of his having killed the woman's man.

She studied Yakima through hard, dark-brown eyes, her fine jaws set in a firm, smooth line. Her nostrils swelled. She drew a deep breath, and her lovely bust rose up higher against her chest.

Her eyes turned even darker as she curled her plump upper, ruby-red lip and, shuttling her gaze to the half-dozen other men in the room, said, "Well, what are you men going to do about it? My husband has been killed in his own establishment, and you all just sit there like hogs in a wallow? Are you men or *mice?*"

With that last, she slapped both her hands down on the creaky balcony rail, gripping the rail as though it were the neck of a chicken she was ringing.

Silence.

The other men in the room glanced back and forth at each other, owl-eyed.

Dread dropped like a cold wheel-hub in the half-breed's belly. Yakima knew what was coming. When a creature like the one standing on the balcony issued a challenge like the one she had just issued, there was no man alive with *cajones* large enough to deny her.

If she'd been ugly, sure. But this woman leaning over the rail just far enough to give every man in the saloon a good shot at the deep, alluringly dark valley between her large, pale breasts was so far from ugly that she couldn't hit ugly with a mountain howitzer.

Yakima looked at the seven other men in the room. They were all looking back at him.

Very slowly, the two men nearest Yakima set the cards they'd been playing facedown on the table. They were both clad in rough trail gear, and they both sported pistols in tied-down holsters. None of the drummers appeared armed though they were all probably carrying hideouts, little poppers tucked away in sleeves or jacket pockets for

19

warding off robbers.

Yakima didn't think he had to worry about them.

The other two men who sat between the drummers and the card players, were hard to figure. One was a long-faced albino wearing the dark-blue attire of a cavalry soldier. The bar on is shoulders made him a first lieutenant. His eyes were a queer yellow beneath the broad brim of his sun-burnished Hardee hat. He was sunk back in his chair, chewing a stove match and staring toward Yakima with a cunning grin.

The beefy, broad-faced man sitting beside him was clad in denim trousers and a checked shirt under a brown leather vest, a salt-crusted tan Stetson on the table beside him. His thick body was turned away from Yakima, facing the bar, but he was looking over his stout left shoulder at the half-breed now, and he had much the same look as his albino friend. His eyes were pale brown and set too close together on either side of a fat, slightly crooked nose. He had about three days worth of dark-brown stubble on his sunburned cheeks.

A brown bottle sat on the table between him and the albino lieutenant. The albino had a quirley between the long, pale, lightly freckled fingers of his left hand, beside a pair of cavalry gloves and gauntlets. His cold, dead eyes gave the lie to his smiling lips that flicked across Yakima, scrutinizing the half-breed thoroughly, mockingly.

It was those two and the two to Yakima's left he had to watch the most closely. Not the drummers though drummers were known to be pistol savvy, as well. And no male of any stripe was immune to the cleavage hanging over the balcony rail.

"Well, what are you waiting for . . . gentlemen?" The woman, who, judging by the smoothness of her skin, was probably in her middle twenties, pitched her voice with a sultry disgust and condemnation.

Yakima held very still, sitting sideways to the wall but gazing into the room, his face implacable, his eyes moving, waiting.

One of the card players, the one sitting sideways to Yakima, turned his head toward the woman. He turned his head slowly back, and his eyes were wide, his chest rising and falling heavily.

Don't, *Yakima silently urged.* She's not worth dyin' for, amigo.

But he was the one who jerked first, all right. And he was the first one to die as Yakima lurched to his feet, swiping his horn-gripped .44 from its holster and drilling the screaming card player between the flaps of his shabby wool vest and through the dead center of the hide tobacco pouch hanging there. He'd leaped to his feet, half-turning toward Yakima, making a perfect target.

But now he was nothing but a blood-spewing, screaming bag of bones as he flew back, triggering his big Russian .44 into the ceiling and flying back against the cold pot-belly stove. His partner hadn't wanted to join his friend's dance—his reluctance was evidence in his suddenly large, gray eyes that were opaque with cold fear—but he'd felt compelled by the fact that his friend had tried it.

And he probably thought that Yakima couldn't get a second shot off as fast as the half-breed did, blowing a quarter-sized hole through the second card player's left eye and into the hand of his partner who was still slumped backward, arms spread, across the stove. Blood and brain matter from the second card player's head splattered across that quivering hand, as well.

Yakima had spied movement out of his right eye.

As he turned, he was vaguely surprised to see that neither the albino cavalry lieutenant nor his beefy partner was making any offensive moves whatever. They merely sat their chairs, grinning shrewdly as before, as though they were watching nude dancers prance around in an opera house.

It was the foolish gamblers who were squirming around, trying to haul out pocket pistols. The man in the orange checked suit had just pulled an ivory gripped, over-and-under derringer from his vest pocket, and was wincing and stumbling backward, cocking one of the hammers, when Yakima punched his ticket with a forty-four caliber round through his upper chest. He slid his smoking Colt toward the drummer standing to the orange-clad man's right, and that gent tossed his own little Smith & Wesson top break .38, which he'd fished out of a shoulder holster beneath his torn tweed coat, onto the table as though it were a scorpion that had fallen onto his lap from the ceiling.

"No, no, no!" he cried, rubbing both hands through his thin, brown hair as he stepped back away from the table, squeezing his eyes closed and closing his hands over his face, as though to ward off a bullet.

Yakima held fire.

He slid the Colt toward the next drummer—a scrawny little man with a bizarrely cherubic face and yellow muttonchop whiskers shaved into arrow points pointing toward his chapped, pink mouth. He just stood there holding a stubby, brass-framed pepperbox revolver pointing toward the floor beside his scuffed, manure-streaked, right halfboot.

He, too, had closed his eyes and was shaking his head from side to side, muttering, "No. No. No. No . . ."

There was a soft thudding sound.

Yakima frowned, looking around. Then he saw the liquid dribbling down from inside the scrawny drummer's right, broadcloth pant leg onto the instep of his right halfboot. The liquid beaded on top of the shoe, and each bead rolled down like a brown ball bearing onto the floor to form a dark pool that was growing on the scarred puncheons.

"No. No. No," he continued mechanically, keeping his eyes closed. "I want no part of this."

"Then you might drop the pepperbox," Yakima suggested.

The man's knobby, little hand opened, and the stubby pinfire pistol dropped to the floor with a clanging thud.

Meanwhile, the first drummer looked down at the hole in his chest, and his eyes acquired a shocked, horrified cast. He placed a hand near the hole, smearing the oozing blood with his fingers.

Then he looked up at Yakima and said in a matter of fact tone devoid of accusing but pitched with mild bewilderment, "You killed me."

"Nope." Yakima shook his head and glanced up at the heavy-breasted Mexican woman staring down over the balcony rail. "She did."

"God damn you," the drummer said with a sob though it was hard to say whom he was addressing, because he'd dropped his shocked gaze to the floor.

His knees buckled and hit the floor. His eyes rolled back into his head. He fell forward onto his face, sighed, shook, and lay still.

Yakima looked around. The albino and the beefy gent

sat as before, as though they'd turned to wax about three minutes ago. The woman stared down from the balcony. She didn't look as angry anymore as perplexed.

"You two ain't playin'?" Yakima asked the last two surviving customers.

"Nah." This from the albino, who slid his matchstick from one side of his mouth to the other, showing the ends of his yellow teeth. "MacElvy done told me about your reputation . . . Yakima Henry."

Yakima frowned at the beefy gent with little eyes set too close together. And then he recognized him. MacElvy hauled his big, beefy frame out of his chair, smiling affably and sweeping a hand through his thick, light-red hair that curled onto his sun-blistered forehead.

"Sergeant MacElvy," he said. "Remember?"

"Yeah," Yakima said, depressing his Colt's hammer but keeping the pistol aimed between the two men, not yet willing to let his guard down. "I remember."

MacElvy had been a line sergeant at Camp Hildebrandt over at Apache Pass, when Yakima had been a civilian scout and tracker at "Fort Hell," as the lonely outpost had been more informally dubbed by those unfortunate enough to have been stationed there, just after Lee had surrendered to Grant at Appomattox courthouse. When he'd accrued more sins than even the frontier, Indian-fighting cavalry, hard pressed to find enough men to throw against Geronimo and the other Apache war chiefs in Arizona, had been able to swallow, MacElvy had been run out of the army in disgrace.

General drunkenness, insubordination, and the maiming of a whore at one of the hog pens near Fort Hell had been only a few of the noncommissioned officers' crimes, as Yakima remembered. It had been ten years since Yakima had worked at Hildebrandt, longer still since he'd last seen MacElvy, but he also remembered the man to be a general lout and no-account who'd actually seemed to have been working *toward* having his chevrons stripped from his uniform sleeves.

MacElvy stood facing Yakima. He was a big, burly gent, as tall as Yakima. He was grinning, narrowing his light brown eyes but the expression was hollow, his face a mask. He smelled as though beer and forty-rod were oozing from his pores on the tails of his sour sweat.

"Been a while since Camp Hell, Henry." MacElvy glanced around the bloody room. "You been busy." He narrowed an eye at the half-breed. "And your reputation precedes you. You've killed your share."

"Only those that needed it."

MacElvy glanced at his albino partner. "Bruno Hilger . . . uh . . . *Lieutenant* Bruno Hilger, that is . . . meet Yakima Henry. One of the best trackers, aside from the Aravaipa scouts, we had at Camp Hell back in the day. Him and his Southern pal, Seth Barksdale."

Hilger gave his chin a cordial dip. "Pleasure."

"All mine."

"Wonder where that old grayback, Barksdale, is now," said MacElvy.

"Probably dead," Yakima said, meaning it. He remembered that his dashing young partner, only a few years older than Yakima, and born and bred on a rich cotton plantation in Georgia, had trod a dangerous course between women, not all of whom had been unattached.

Yakima hadn't heard from Seth in six, seven years. If he wasn't dead, he'd probably gone back to his family's plantation to live the life of Southern-style luxury, fishing for catfish, a basket of fried chicken by his side, a tumbler of corn liquor in hand, a busty, beribboned Southern belle clad in crinoline sprawled on a blanket beneath a mossy oak.

MacElvy laughed. "What brings you to Horsetooth?"

Yakima shrugged. "Nothin' to speak of. What brings you to Horsetooth?"

MacElvy studied him with a faint, fleeting suspicion in his eyes. Then he laughed. "Same as you, I reckon. Nothin'!" He patted Yakima's stout right shoulder, hitched his denims higher on his broad hips. "Nice to see ya again, Henry. That was some right fancy shootin'. I reckon them stories I heard about you weren't stretchin'

27

things much. Well ... anyway ..." He glanced at Hilger. "I reckon we'd best pull our picket pines, eh, Lieutenant? Get on back to the post?"

Still seated, Hilger was studying Yakima with much the same look that MacElvy had worn, only Hilger's look wasn't nearly as fleeting as the former Sergeant's.

"I said," MacElvy said, raising his voice and giving the Lieutenant a commanding look, "we'd best get on back to the post—eh, Lieutenant?"

"Right," said Hilger, rising and adjusting the angle of his hat over his pale, washed-out eyes, his long, coarse, white hair hanging straight down past his collar.

He picked up his gloves and gauntlets, fished a pair of rectangular, rose-lensed sunglasses out of his tunic pocket, donned the spectacles, and walked to the saloon's batwings. He was a tall man, Yakima saw now. Taller than either he or MacElvy, but he probably weighed only a hundred and forty, fifty pounds still dripping wet from a bath.

MacElvy pinched his hat brim to Yakima, winked, and followed the Lieutenant outside.

When they were gone, Yakima found himself staring at the saloon owner's wife, now a widow, standing at the bottom of the stairs. She was looking around at the devastation and pensively fingering a gold locket hanging from a gold chain around her long, pretty neck.

3

"You're a hard man to kill," the barman's widow said, strolling toward Yakima while continuing to finger the locket hanging to just above her cleavage.

Yakima knew he should take his bottle, mount up, and ride into the desert. Trouble had a way of dogging him. It had dogged him here. He tried to keep one step ahead of it. But he couldn't take his eyes off the splendid creature walking toward him, letting her mud-brown eyes flick from his head to his boots and back again and then across the broad stretch of his powerful shoulders straining the top buttons of his black and red calico shirt.

"My condolences," Yakima said.

She stopped before him, glanced down at the horn-gripped revolver angled across his left hip. "You are a *pistolero*."

"Sometimes."

She arched a brow. Her cheeks were perfectly sculpted, rounded, not at all severe, and her eyes were a deep, luminous brown. They glittered in the trapezoids of copper, mote-shot light angling through the windows and casting sharp-edged shadows onto the floor. Her wavy, raven hair was very long, and down here where he could see her better, it fairly glowed with a bluish undertone. Where the light did not reach, the room was all purple shadows swarming with flies that had already found the freshly spilled blood and dead meat.

Her lips were full. Bee-stung, some would call them. And cherry-red. Her skin was the off-white of almond butter. If it were any darker, she would not be allowed in her husband's saloon. She was not very tall, but she was curved in ways to make a man want to cut his own head off with a rusty saw. The faint smell of sandalwood and wild cherry blossoms that hovered around her freshly bathed body enhanced her primitive allure.

Behind the wild urges she evoked in him—would evoke in any man, young, old, or half-dead—Yakima was trying to figure out what in hell she'd been doing, married to a pig like Clancy.

"An outlaw?" she asked, her eyes flicking once more across his chest.

"Only when necessary."

"The man mentioned you were an army scout at

Fort Hildebrandt."

"Awhile back."

"And a tracker."

Yakima frowned. "What does that have to do with—?"

"Why don't we sit down and have a drink?" she said, cutting him off and dropping lithely into the extra chair at his table.

She crossed her legs beneath her skirt, the skirt drawing taut against them, outlining the curve of each knee and thigh in turn. He couldn't help imagining what they would look like without the skirt, wrapped around his back.

It had been a long ride down from Colorado . . .

There was only one glass. She filled it with tequila from his bottle, held the glass up to her lips, sniffed, ran the rim against the underside of her bottom lip, and then very slowly closed her upper lip over the rim, and sipped.

She swallowed, pressing her lips together. Her throat moved, and he heard the faint sound of the liquid dropping down her throat. There was a faint sheen of moisture on her mouth as she stared up at him through those brown eyes beneath her coal-black brows.

Yakima scowled down at her, baffled, "You always drink with men who shoot your husbands?"

"Clancy was my first," she said with an offhand air, glancing pensively over her shoulder to where her deceased husband could not be seen sprawled behind the bar. "I'd never intended to marry, but I guess there's just no stopping true love . . . once it gets ahold on you."

She gave a half-smile, half-slitting her eyes, and he couldn't make up his mind if she'd been serious or not. It was hard to imagine such a succulent creature as she falling in love with a pugnacious old dog like Clancy, who had to have been nearly twice her age.

"I'm Paloma," she said. "Paloma Collado. Formerly"— she glanced again toward the bar—"Brewer." She smiled. "Please, sit down."

Yakima kicked his chair to adjust it, and then sagged slowly into it, still studying her, scowling, wondering what Paloma Collado's game was. A voice in his head told him to take the bottle and ride. *Leave* the bottle and ride. But his feet would not comply.

Holding his gaze and smiling a little brighter, causing a hot knife of unfettered desire to twist in his heart, she slid her glass across the table to him. He could see the faint smudge where she'd pressed her lips to it.

The knife twisted.

Boots thumped above the sound of occasional horse and wagon traffic outside the saloon, along the main street of the little Arizona desert town of Horsetooth. Yakima slid his hand to the horn grips of his .44 but kept the revolver in its holster as a big, bull-legged man in a tattered canvas coat and equally tattered canvas hat ambled into the saloon, sweating. Brown-streaked pewter hair curled to his coat collar, and a walrus mustache of the same color framed his mouth.

He stopped just inside the batwings, glowered down toward where the dead men lay before him, and then slid that glowering, confounded gaze toward Yakima and the young widow. Something else must have caught his eye, because now he stepped to his right and canted his head to stare down at the floor behind the bar.

"Ho-lee shit!" He doffed his hat and scratched the back of his head. "I *thought* I heard gunshots. I was takin' a nap back at my . . . Miss Paloma, do you realize that Clancy is layin' dead back here? At least . . ." He ambled back behind the bar and made a jerky, twisting movement that was followed by a soft thud, telling Yakima he'd kicked the barman's body over. "Yep, he's dead, all right. Dead as a post."

"Yes, it's a tragedy, Marshal Wade. Would you haul the bodies over to the undertaker's for me, please? There are two more over here." Paloma glanced toward the first two men—the card players—whom Yakima had dispatched.

From behind the bar, and scratching the back of his head again, the Marshal, who appeared to be pushing a hard-earned fifty, said, "Well, who done all this *killin'?*"

"They all shot each other," Paloma said, keeping

her eyes on Yakima. "Those two there grabbed me in a most humiliating way, and Clancy, being the good, devoted husband he was, tried to intervene with his shotgun, and took a bullet for his trouble. The other two—over there—decided to get involved on my behalf, and they all just shot hell out of each other. A tragedy. I'm devastated."

The cool beauty splashed more tequila into the glass and threw back half of it before sliding the glass back toward Yakima. "I'm having a drink to calm my nerves. This gentleman was kind enough to share his bottle."

The town marshal stared at Yakima suspiciously. "Ain't that nice of him . . ."

"Please, Marshal Wade," Paloma urged. "Just clear the place. I'm sure whatever these men have in their pockets will more than pay for their burial."

The marshal sighed, shook his head, and shrugged. "If you say so . . ."

The big, sloppy gent ambled out from behind the bar and pushed through the batwings. He stopped on the front porch, stuck a finger of each hand in his mouth, and loosed a shrill whistle. "Albert, Johnny—get your worthless asses over here and clear these cadavers out of the saloon. Your pa's got business!"

Presently, the marshal moved back into the saloon with two thick-set, raw-boned, young, overall-clad men, both smelling like fresh horse shit, on his heels. Their clothes were liberally smeared with dung. The boys had the blank stares and awkward, halting gaits of half-wits. They both glanced with mute interest at Miss Paloma and the big half-breed sitting at the table against the far wall, both sipping tequila from the same glass.

"Well, I didn't call ya in here to mooncalf around," the marshal said, gesturing with his arm. "Haul them dead men outta here and over to your daddy's livery stable. There's another one, ole Clancy himself, behind the bar. Whatever you find in their pockets belongs to your pa. Tell him he owes me a beer and steak and a free shoein'."

The big, sloppy marshal, who'd likely been a cow puncher at one time before getting too old for the strenuous work, leaned against the bar while the boys cleared the place of the bloody cadavers, one taking the legs, the other the arms and shoulders.

While the boys did the heavy lifting, the marshal leaned back against the bar, poked at his teeth with a shaved matchstick, and studied Yakima and Paloma with a skeptical, befuddled expression. The pretty widow and the man who'd widowed her said nothing until the place was cleared and the boys and the marshal had left, the marshal calling out his condolences over his shoulder as the batwings clattered back into place behind him.

"I didn't think they'd ever leave," Paloma told Yakima.

His heart was thudding in his temples. His throat was dry. He cleared it, swallowed.

"Me, neither."

"Would you like to join me upstairs?"

"No."

She threw back the last half-inch of tequila in the bottom of the shot glass, licked her lips, and smiled. "But you're going to."

"Hell, yes."

She placed one of her hands on his, leaning forward slightly, pressing her full bosom against the side of the table. Wrapping her hand around his, she rose.

He slid his chair back and rose, as well, and let her lead him across the room to the uncarpeted stairs. As they climbed the stairs, the staircase creaking beneath them, the sounds from the street dwindling as they rose toward the second story, that voice in Yakima's head was growing more fervid but it, too, was fading as though into the distance.

Desire sharpened by dread touched him like an ice pick to the loins. The girl's hand was soft and small in his own. She was flexing her fingers, and the slight pressure of her flesh against his enflamed him further.

"Nothing good would come of this," he told himself.

"Not one damn bit of good, you stupid, good-for-nothin' half-breed. In fact, you'll be lucky to get out of here alive."

Still, he thought, looking down at the girl walking up the steps beside him, her bosom rising and falling behind the low-cut dress . . . what a way to go!

***

The muffled crack of a distant pistol woke him.

He jerked his head up from his pillow, and instinctively reached for the Colt hanging from a chair beside the woman's bed.

"No," she said, groaning as she too awoke from her post-coital slumber. "It's just . . . someone over at the Mexican cantina on the other side of town. It's crawling with banditos over there." Her voice was deep and raspy. She clawed at his back, trying to draw him back down to where she sprawled naked on the sheets still damp and hot from their ravenous coupling.

Yakima released the pistol. He looked at the two wooden balcony doors thrown open to catch a breeze in hopes of relieving the fierce desert heat. When he and the girl had finally separated and slumbered from exhaustion, the sun had not quite set.

Now, it was good dark. Stars shimmered in the sky above the village of Horsetooth. This side of town was quiet, but he could hear men's and women's voices raised in raucous revelry to the south—straight out from the hotel/saloon that now had only a single owner.

"The Mexican part of town," the girl said, nibbling his arm. He could feel her hot tongue and the dull ends of her teeth. "Let them all kill each other, give us some peace and quiet."

She was running one hand across his back while she nuzzled his arm. Her hair felt coarse as a mare's tail where it touched his skin, lifting chicken flesh.

Yakima blinked sleep from his eyes, cleared his throat, looked down at her where she was pressing her cheek against his bicep, staring up at him with dark, erotic eyes, her mussed hair framing her ivory face.

"How in the hell did you come to marry Clancy?"

"I told you."

"Bullshit. You couldn't love him anymore than I could love the grizzly this necklace came from." He glanced at the claw necklace still hanging down from his stout, red neck and which he'd fashioned from the claws of a bear that had attacked him, nearly killed him, not all that long ago.

She looked down. "It was a marriage of . . . convenience. I was an orphan. I needed a man. Preferably, a wealthy man. So, judge me. I married Clancy because he had money. The saloon is successful though I know it doesn't look like it. He never put much back into it. That was fine with me. More for myself when he kicked the bucket."

Yakima chuckled. "Now, you're talkin'."

She pressed her moist, silky lips to his bicep that bulged like a wheel hub. "Come back down here and make love to me again. I am twenty-three, and Clancy was the only man I ever had. Rest assured, you are the first man who has ever . . . come back here, damn you!"

Yakima had risen, running his hands through his long, sweat-damp hair. The room was as hot a desert jailhouse, and it smelled like sex and sweat. "Gotta get some air."

He didn't bother grabbing his underwear, just his makings sack. He stumbled out the open balcony doors and collapsed into a wicker chair that sat beside a small whicker table, against the wall to the left of the open doors.

"You're a bastard!" she yelled behind him.

"You're gonna kill me," he laughed, leaning forward, elbows on his knees.

"Wouldn't it be a sweet death?" she said in a pouting, little girl's voice.

"Leave me alone. Gotta catch my breath."

She threw a pillow. It landed just inside the doors and skidded out onto the balcony. Ignoring her, Yakima opened the hide pouch and withdrew chopped tobacco and wheat papers, and rolled a tight quirley. He removed a match from a box inside the pouch, struck it to life on the floor, and touched it to the cigarette.

He flipped the match over the balcony rail and into the street that was dark save one saloon across the street to his left. Lantern light pushed out through the open windows, but it was fairly quiet over there. It was probably around ten, maybe eleven o'clock, and the whores were probably entertaining their customers in their rooms.

The hot, dry desert air was scented with the smell of mesquite smoke and frijoles remaining from supper fires.

Yakima leaned forward, elbows on his knees, smoking and staring over the rail and into the night. Her soft tread sounded behind him, and she stopped between the open, roughhew doors, naked, long hair hanging down her back and curling around her sides to her flat belly.

4

"We need a breeze," she said, and slumped onto his lap, resting her head against his neck.

He hooked his right arm around her, liking the feel of her. It had been a long time since he'd had a woman. Not since Denver. There'd been no time for women on the trail, as he had a couple of lawdogs after him. Turned out he'd killed a brother of one of the lawdogs, and, though the dead man had been trying to steal Yakima's horse, the lawman, a local sheriff from Colorado Territory, had wanted to see the half-breed hang.

He looked at the girl slumped against him. His mouth quirked a wry smile as he ran his gaze down one of her slim arms to her crossed legs hanging down off his knee.

Out of the frying pan and into the fire . . .

What was her game?

She turned her face to him, kissed his cheek. When

that got no reaction, she stuck her tongue in his ear. Then she dropped her hand between his legs, and she smiled at him shrewdly.

Yakima groaned.

"You are much hombre," she said, plying her magic.

He stiffened. The cigarette burned down to his fingers, and he dropped it. She cooed in his ear while her hand did its dance. Yakima leaned back, stretched his lips back from his teeth, groaned, and shuddered.

"It is nice, giving you pleasure," she whispered.

Yakima didn't say anything. He felt spent and dreamy.

"Do you like me?"

"What's not to like?"

"How much do you like me?"

"How much do I need to like you?"

She smiled. "A lot."

Time to leave, he thought. Go. *Now!*

Voices rose from the far side of the street. Shadows moved behind the batwing doors of the saloon, and Yakima glimpsed a blue Hardee hat and cavalry tunic. He also recognized the brawny frame of Edgar MacElvy just before he and Lieutenant Hilger pushed through the doors and stepped out into the inky darkness of the street.

They were laughing drunkenly, boots clomping off down the boardwalk, away from Yakima and Paloma. She'd sat up now, straddling the half-breed's knee, and was staring out over the balcony rail, turning her head slowly, tracking the drunken pair.

"What's wrong?" Yakima asked.

"Them. They've been snooping around here for days now. I wish they'd go back to their outpost like they said."

"Why do you suppose they've been snooping around?"

"Who knows?" Paloma hiked her bare shoulder. "They are snoops." She turned to him. "Anyway, they are gone now. Too drunk to cause any trouble tonight. Are you hungry?"

"Nah." Between bouts in her large, four-poster bed, she'd gone downstairs and brought up four beef burros and beans and a fresh bottle of mescal. "Just tired."

"Me, too. You're the kind of man who wears a girl out." She slipped off his knee, leaving it hot and moist where she'd been sitting, and jerked his arm. "Come on—let's go to sleep."

Suddenly, he was even more tired than he'd thought he was. All the lovemaking, the good food, and forty-rod were tugging hard on his eyelids. The bed sounded good. He rose, wrapped his arms around her, and kissed her, liking the pliant way she kissed him back and ran her fingers lightly down his shoulder blades, causing chicken flesh to rise once more.

He'd sleep in her bed tonight, because he was too tired to find another even if he'd been strong enough to tear himself away from this Spanish succubus. He was curious about what she wanted from him. That she wanted something was obvious. He was a stranger who'd killed her husband, and she'd made love to him like the most gifted, best-paid whore in the toniest New Orleans brothel.

But he no longer wanted to know. Whatever it was, it was trouble, just as she was trouble.

The worst kind of trouble. Woman trouble.

He'd ride out first thing in the morning and cross the border into Mexico around noon.

He followed her inside and flopped down in the bed. She folded up with her smooth, warm butt pressed up against his groin, pulled his arm around her, taking his hand in both of hers and holding it very tightly to her breasts.

Sometime later he woke to see her dressing stealthily in the room's thick shadows, her jostling hair glinting dully in the cool, blue light of dawn. She was trying to make no noise, he could tell. He could hear her tight, little breaths. She was breathing hard, anxiously. She dropped a serape over her shoulders, plucked a brown sombrero off a wall peg, and carried her boots out the door and closed the door softly behind her. He heard her bare feet on the steps. She wasn't going to put her boots on until she was downstairs. That's how badly she wanted him to keep sleeping.

Yakima sighed and sat up, raked his hands through his hair.

What was she up to?

"Push on, fool," he grumbled aloud. "Saddle Wolf and ride for the border."

Knowing that what he *should* do and what he *would* do were polar opposites, he dressed and headed outside just as she rode out from behind the saloon and hotel on a short, rangy Mexican blue. She wore a striped serape, with a thin scarf wrapped around the lower part of her face, beneath the brown sombrero, as though she did not want to be recognized. Fortunately, she did not look toward the saloon's front porch but spurred the mount down the street in the opposite direction.

In seconds, she was hunkered low over the blue's neck, and she and the mustang were galloping toward the end of town like a bat out of hell. They followed a bend to the right, and the morning shadows consumed them, the thuds of the horse's galloping hooves dwindling quickly beneath the raucous chirping of the morning birds.

Yakima headed over to the livery barn and in less than five minutes he was saddled up and galloping on out of the morning-quiet town in the direction the woman had gone. He had no problem trailing her. Her hoof prints were the freshest ones on the wagon trail that curved through the desert, meandering around low bluffs and boulder snags, creosote shrubs stretching their long, bristly tendrils from both sides of the trail.

He hadn't been on the trail long before he spied movement ahead.

Paloma was galloping up a long, gentle incline ahead of Yakima and gradually curving to his right, which was south. She was merely a brown and black blur from this distance of a half a mile, but it had to be her.

She was angling up the shoulder of a sawtooth, sandstone ridge that was glowing copper now as the sun broke free of the horizon and began sliding its buttery light across the bristling chaparral, stretching long, slender shadows toward the west sides of shrubs and rocks. Larger, darker shadows stretched away from the walls of dykes and mesas.

When Yakima had gained the top of the sandstone ridge, he saw the woman riding the blue up the side of another, low hill to the southwest. She'd slowed her mount considerably since she'd left town, but Yakima hadn't. She was only a hundred or so yards ahead of him.

She was pulling the blue up toward an ancient, brown adobe church that sat atop the broad, sandy crest of the hill and which was ringed with the remains of an old, mostly abandoned Mexican village. Yakima knew the place, for he'd taken this trail in and out of Mexico many times in the past, and stopped for water provided by the well of the congenial old padre who ran the church.

He touched spurs to Wolf's flanks and galloped on the down the ridge. At the bottom, he swung off the main trail and followed a slender game trail along the side of a bristling, boulder-choked wash that ran along the northwestern base of the bluff that the church and the village perched on.

As he rode, he scared up several cactus wrens and a couple of turkey buzzards that had been feeding on some dead thing in the wash, and he gnashed his teeth together, hoping the birds hadn't given his presence away to the woman.

He followed the game trail about three-quarters of the way up the ridge and stopped his white-socked, black stallion in a shady place where mesquites and sycamores pushed up around a gravelly seep. Yakima threw Wolf's reins perfunctorily over a branch—the horse had been trained to stay wherever its reins hung—and clambered to the top of the bluff.

Crouching low behind a boulder, he saw Paloma just then riding into the barren yard of the church. Yakima was flanking the church's northeast corner, so she was sort of riding toward both him and the front of the church, the morning sunshine glistening beautifully in her coal-black hair that was still beguiling mussed from their lovemaking.

The padre's shack, constructed of adobe bricks and vertical mesquite rails, sat to the right of the church, which fronted several dilapidated outbuildings. One was a chicken coop. Chickens from the coop were out foraging in the yard, and they squawked and scattered now as the girl drew up to the well that sat in the middle of the yard.

The padre himself was just then stepping off the stoop of his humble shack. He was clad in a calico smock belted with rope around his bulging waist, and canvas trousers and rope-soled sandals. His coarse, gray-brown hair hung in a long braid down his back.

He donned his ratty, straw sombrero as he walked out toward where the woman was dismounting her horse, patting the blue's neck appreciatively. Yakima took advantage of the morning shadows and the tufts of brush and rocks for partial concealment as he ran, crouching, toward the padre's cabin. As he did, he saw the padre spread his arms out, palms up, and by the sound of his voice, he was not happy about the woman's visit.

Yakima crouched behind a pile of rocks bristling with cactus off one corner of the priest's hovel. From here, he could see around the left side of the shack and into the yard, where the woman and the priest were talking while the blue drew water from a bucket she'd winched up from the well.

Yakima couldn't hear what they were saying, but the

BLOOD OF THE HORSETOOTH WIDOW

priest continued to throw his arms up and out, as though he were arguing. Finally, the woman stepped around him and began striding for the shack.

Yakima ducked down behind the pile of rocks, and when the woman and the priest were both out of sight in front of the cabin, the half-breed darted out away from the rocks and, running nearly silently on his moccasin-clad feet, dashed to the hovel's back wall.

He crept around the left rear corner and now he could see through a window of the tiny shack the priest saying, " . . . well enough for a visit. I told you to wait at least a week, Paloma."

They were speaking Spanish, but Yakima understood enough to catch the jist of what they were saying.

"I want to see my one true love, Padre Giuseppe. Is that so hard to understand?" The woman's voice had a mocking, condescending tone.

"Your one true love. That's a crock, Paloma!"

"Out of the way, Padre! You wouldn't want me to inform your superiors in Durango that your brother is the notorious bandito, Octavio La Paz—would you?"

Yakima felt his jaw drop.

The name Octavio La Paz had been notorious both north and south of the border for a long time. The half-breed had heard off and on over the years that the man was dead only to hear again that he'd robbed a large mine or a gold shipment in the border country. Once it was said he'd killed several Chiricahuas in cold blood, fanning the flames of the Southwestern Apaches wars. The wars were a great way to divert attention from his savage outlawry.

"You are the devil's sister," the priest told the woman. "And to think that I warned you about getting mixed up with *mi hermano* back when you started . . . when you started stepping out on your husband. Now, I realize it was Octavio I should have warned against taking up with the likes of *you*, Senora Brewer."

"It's Collado once again, Padre." Yakima couldn't see the woman, but he could tell from her tone that she was grinning. Sneering. "My beloved husband fell pretty to a big *mestizo* faster with a pistol than Clancy was with his shotgun. A tragedy. I will be in morning for weeks!" She chuckled.

"The devil's sister," said the priest in a bewildered, crestfallen tone.

A third, weaker voice rose from the other side of the cabin and probably another room, judging by the muffled quality. "Giuseppe, I am awake. Send her in."

There was a slapping sound, as though the priest had let his arms drop to his sides in defeat. "You heard him," he told the girl. "He's awake. But he is very weak. He lost a lot of blood when the Apaches scalped him. He needs his sleep to fight the infection. Mind what I say.

50

He might be a bandido, but he is still my brother and I will not let you . . .."

The priest let his voice trail off. Apparently, Paloma had left the room. Yakima had heard the clomping of her boots dwindling off to the opposite side of the shack. Yakima retraced his steps to the back of the cabin and followed the sound of voices to a window on the other side of the back door.

"There you are, *mi amore!*" the woman said. "How are you feeling?"

"How does it look like I am feeling?" came the sickly male voice. "You should try being scalped sometime. It is the most pleasant feeling in the world!"

The bandito sobbed miserably.

"And my eye. Oh, my poor eye. Those heathens stuck a hot poker in it and left me to suffer and die!"

Paloma made a hissing sound.

Yakima dropped to one knee beside the window, doffing his hat so the crown wouldn't be seen through the closed curtain buffeting slightly in the breeze, and heard her say, "I am so sorry, Octavio, you poor wretch!" A pause. "And . . . the money . . .?"

The man gave a groaning sigh. "I won't be able to go back for it for quite sometime, if ever. I'm miserable. I certainly can't sit a horse."

Octavio La Paz sobbed again, sucked a rattling breath.

There was a creaking sound. Yakima knew that Paloma had sat down on the bed beside her lover. The half-breed vaguely wondered how many she had, and felt foolish for feeling an annoying rake of jealousy.

But that's what a night like the one he'd just spent with a woman like Paloma Collado, formerly Brewer, would do to a man.

Turn him into a foolish mooncalf.

He snarled and closed his hand over the grips of his Colt.

5

Get a grip on yourself, *Yakima told himself.* You spent one night with the woman, and look what she's got you doing. Like a simpering idiot, you've followed her out to some other man's cabin. You're acting like a twelve-year-old boy with a schoolyard crush!

He wanted to leave. Not only the alluring woman but the name of her legendary lover—Octavio La Paz—held him in place beneath the notorious bandito's window.

She was saying just beyond the open window, "You have no choice but to tell me where the payroll money is, now, *mi amore.* I alone you can trust. The others were going to double-cross you; if you hadn't taken the loot from them, they would have taken it from you."

With an air of desperation, La Paz said, "You haven't seen any of them, have you? *Jorgenson?* In my condition, I'm a sitting duck out here!"

"No, no, no, *mi amore*—I have not seen Jorgenson or any of the others." Yakima wished she'd quit calling him her lover. "I assure you that if I do, you will be the first to know. I will come to you first. And I don't care what they threaten me with . . . or what they may promise me, if it comes to that . . . I will never tell them where you are!"

Yakima had to choke back a snicker. She was playing La Paz like a well-tuned mandolin.

"You wouldn't do that, would you?" begged the one-eyed Octavio La Paz. "After all we've meant to each other this past year?"

"Shhhh," said Paloma. "Lie back down, now, *mi amore*. You're getting overwrought. Look there, sweat is breaking out on your forehead." There was the tinkle of water being wrung from a cloth into a washbowl. "There. Now, why don't you tell me where you buried the payroll money. I know someone I can trust to help me fetch it for you. For us. Once we have the money, we will go down to Mexico City. There, we will get you the very best doctors and find a master carver who will whittle you a new eye almost as good as the one the Apaches took from you."

Again, there was the sound of the cloth being wrung out.

"I am . . . I am not so sure. I want to, but . . . ."

"Octavio, don't tell me that after this wonderful year we spent together, all the thrilling and joyous trysts, fooling around behind my pig of a husband's foolish back, you don't *trust* me!"

"It is not that, *mi amore*," La Paz said. "It is that I don't want to endanger your life, Paloma. You have no idea the savagery of the other men in my gang. Jorgenson and Cordoba alone are wildcats! If they followed you into the desert, you might never come back. Believe me, they're out there looking for the loot they would have taken from me if I hadn't taken it from them first!"

"Shhh, shhh, *shhhhhh!* There you go again, my darling. You must rest easier, don't get your blood up. Like I said, I have found a man who can help me. One very capable of guiding me into the desert and protecting me from all that might be out there. And rest assured you can trust him. He is big, somewhat savage, and, while good with a gun, a little dunderheaded. Such a man is good at taking orders . . . and respecting a girl's wishes."

With that last, Yakima could hear the grin in her voice. His cheeks burned with indignation. She'd played him for the same kind of fool she'd played La Paz for . . .

"How did you meet this man?" La Paz asked, his voice pitched with suspicion.

"He killed Clancy."

"What?"

"He did us both a favor. Now, we can be together . . . after I've retrieved the loot."

"How do I know you will not run off with this hombre? This big savage, as you call him."

Paloma laughed. "Dear heart, he is as ugly as a dog. In fact, he even has fangs. And he is cow-stupid, but he knows the desert. He was once a tracker and scout at Fort Hildebrandt. No, mi amore, I could never have feelings for such a big, dumb, ugly desert rat. He will help me retrieve the loot, nothing more. And when we have no more use for him . . . ."

La Paz chuckled, but there was a skeptical tone to the laughter. "You must bring him to me. I must meet this man and make sure he knows who he is dealing with . . . and what will happen to him if he chooses to deceive me."

Yakima felt his lips raise a satisfied smile.

How was she going to meet this obstacle?

Head on, it turned out.

In a soft, sensual voice, she said, "*Mi amore*, there is no time for that. That white-haired cavalry Lieutenant, the *albino,* and his friend, MacElvy, have been hanging around the saloon. I think they suspect something. I took a chance riding out here this morning. I meant to come earlier but . . . I guess I was more tired than I realized. Don't worry," she added quickly. "I made sure I was not followed."

Again, Yakima had to choke back a dry snicker. Paloma was good at many things but making sure she wasn't followed wasn't one of them.

"Trust me, my darling," she said, in an even softer, more sensual voice. It sounded as though she was nuzzling the man's neck or perhaps a lower area. "Please, trust me. I want so much for us to be together." There was the quiet rustle of sheets being slid around. "The only way . . . for that to happen, however . . . as you well know . . . is if we have enough money for us to make our escape . . . together."

Throatily, La Paz said, "You expect me to believe that you could still love me now . . . ugly wretch that I am?"

Silence.

La Paz groaned throatily.

Yakima's ear tips warmed.

After awhile, La Paz said, his voice slightly pinched, "Find me some paper. I will draw you a map."

"Padre!" Paloma shouted, shattering the intimate quiet. "A pad of paper. *Hurry!*"

Yakima waited, pressing his back against the adobe bricks of the priest's shack, a skeptical scowl on his face. There wasn't much more to hear for a while. He assumed that La Paz was sketching a map to where he'd hid the army payroll loot. The priest was stomping around in the front of the shack, grumbling, but finally stalked out the front door.

Yakima worried that La Paz's more devout brother

might head this way, but was relieved when he didn't hear the slap and scuff of the older man's sandals.

"I think that's right," La Paz told Paloma in Spanish, sounding fatigued now from the woman's visit and her ministrations. There was a clink as though of a pencil being dropped on the floor, and the ripping of a leaf from a notepad. "The X there marks where I buried the money when the trackers from Fort Bryce were bearing down on me. Them on one side, Jorgenson to the other side, with the Apaches hovering over us all from the ridges."

He gave a ragged sigh and another liquid sob. "At least, the Apaches massacred the trackers. If only they would have done the same to Jorgenson and his little friend, Cordoba."

The infamous bandito chuckled with devilish delight. He clipped the laughter with a groan. "They'd done their damage, though. I was hurt too bad to go back for the loot. You'll have to do it. I trust you, Paloma. See to it I can trust both you and this stupid savage you've signed up to guide you into the desert."

"Don't worry. He knows who he is working for, *mi amore*. He trembled at the sound of your name. He stopped trembling when I promised that you would pay him handsomely."

"Be very careful, my dear Paloma. Many hazards out there in the desert, the Chiricahuas not the least of them!"

"Please, do not worry about me, my love," Paloma said. "Here, have a drink of this. It will make you feel better."

"What is it?"

"Mescal. Fresh from Mexico. I bought a barrel of it from traders last week."

"Ahhh," La Paz said. "Paloma, you are as thoughtful as you are beautiful."

She giggled.

Yakima rolled his eyes.

There was the gurgling sound of La Paz drinking the mescal. The gurgling stopped. The outlaw smacked his lips, sighed. "Ah, that hits the spo—*awwwwwww-chhht-t-t-chh!*"

Yakima frowned, glanced sidelong at the window from which violent strangling sounds emanated.

La Paz croaked out in Spanish, "Wha . . . what did .... *achhhhhh-achhhhhhh!* . . . did you put in . . .? *Achhh-hh-achhhh!*"

Paloma giggled. "Snakeroot, mi amore. Boiled up and strained, it blends very well with the mescal, does it not?"

"My . . . eyeballs . . . *achhhhh-achhhhh-awwwwwck-kkkkkkk* . . . are . . . exploding . . . *help!*" He wasn't able to raise his voice very loudly.

"So that's how it feels. I always wondered. I was going to give some to Clancy when he was no longer useful. My new man saved me the trouble." Paloma laughed. "Thanks for the map. I do hope it won't take you too long to die, mi amore. *Dios,* you do look awful. I swear your head has swollen to twice its size, and I didn't think an hombre's face could ever get *that* red!"

"Awckkkkkkkk-awcckkkkkkkkk-awckkkkkkk-kawhkkkkkkk!"

"Good bye, you fool," Paloma said. "Sleep well."

Yakima heard only the strident clomping of her boots on the shack's stone floor. They faded quickly beneath the violent strangling, choking, and retching sounds of the soon-to-be-expired Octavio La Paz.

Yakima moved away from the window and looked around the side of the shack toward the front yard. Paloma was strolling toward where she'd left her horse. The priest was trimming some transplanted and irrigated rose bushes growing up from a bed of rich, black dirt lined with rocks and which sheathed a shrine of some sort.

"Better see to your brother, padre," the woman said, stepping into the Mexican blue's saddle. "I think he might have caught something in his throat."

Laughing, she neck-reined the horse around and galloped out of the yard.

As the priest started running toward the shack, Yakima drew back behind the hovel's back wall. He stared off, in hang-jawed shock at the girl's vileness and pluck.

"That there is one evil little bitch!"

As Octavio La Paz continued to strangle even more violently than before, Yakima jogged back toward where he'd left his horse.

He no longer cared if the priest saw him, which was doubtful, anyway, as the priest was probably trying futilely to administer to his hard-dying brother. Yakima ran straight out from the corner of the shack, dropped down the backside of the bluff, and swung up onto his black stallion's back.

Wolf whickered curiously.

"I told you, partner," Yakima said as he booted the horse on down the slope, "there are wicked women in this world and then there are *wicked* women! Even more wicked than some men I've known." The horse lunged on down the slope, loosing rocks in his wake. "But that one back there—that one gets the ribbon!"

He only wished he could take his own advice.

But, against his own will, he could not. Especially, now, for some damn reason he wasn't entirely sure about.

Maybe it was due to the fact that Paloma Collado was just so insanely beautiful and . . . well, insane. There was something inexplicably intoxicating and compelling about a ravishing young woman who could make such sweet heavenly love to the man who'd killed her husband and then ride out at dawn of the next day to entice her notorious outlaw lover into drawing her a map to his stolen loot—*and then to poison the poor son of a bitch!*

Maybe Yakima was just curious about what exactly she was made of, and what she'd do next. What else did he have to do except head to Mexico to lay low from the American law and look for some menial job to see him through the winter?

This was a hell of a lot more exciting than that!

What he founded himself intending was to intercept her where the game trail diverged from the main one, and see how she'd play it . . . him . . . if for so no other reason than for entertainment, though he fully realized that playing with diamondbacks would likely be a whole lot healthier.

He swung Wolf onto the main trail, and stopped him.

Yakima stared toward the southeast, which was the direction from which Paloma should be heading toward him shortly.

The sun had climbed high. It hammered down on the trail. Insects buzzed in the arroyos around him. That was the only sound until the woman's scream cleaved the heavy, mid-morning silence and set the half-breed's pulse to throbbing in his ears.

6

The half-breed gave Wolf the steel, and the black stallion lunged into an instant gallop.

The black gained the top of the first hill to the east, and barreled down the other side. It ran to the top of another higher hill and blasted past the turn off to the large, brown church mounted atop the bluff on Yakima's left and where, if the bandito was lucky, Octavio La Paz had drifted on over the Divide.

When the desert leveled off, Yakima checked down the black, stopping him and turning him sideways to the trail. Ahead, three horses were galloping off in the opposite direction, heading off away from the main trail and angling through the chaparral, heading toward a range of dun mountains rising in the south. They were blurry streaks from this distance of two hundred yards or so, trailing plumes of adobe-colored dust.

Yakima reached back and pulled his spyglass from one of his saddlebag pouches. Telescoping the brass-plated piece, he raised it to his right eye and adjusted the focus until the three horses and three riders swam into clarified view.

The lead rider, on a bay horse, wore the blue uniform of the frontier cavalry. Bruno Hilger. The large man riding beside him wore rough, earth-toned range gear, and a high-crowned black hat. Paloma was mounted in front of Edgar MacElvy, whose bulk all but hid the woman, but Yakima could see her long, blue-black hair flying out behind both hers and MacElvy's right shoulders as they galloped hell-for-leather toward the dun line of craggy peaks ahead of them. Her sombrero blew out in the wind, as well, fixed to her neck by the chin thong.

Hilger was trailing Paloma's Mexican blue by the horse's bridle reins.

Yakima scowled after the retreating horses and riders. The woman had been right. The men had been snooping around for a reason. They must have suspected that Paloma had been in cahoots with the banditos who'd robbed the army payroll. They'd likely been keeping an even closer watch on her than she'd realized.

Now her goose was cooked.

She may have fooled La Paz into giving her the map to the stolen loot, but now the only two it was doing any good was the albino cavalry lieutenant, Hilger, and the belligerent former sergeant who'd been kicked out of the cavalry in disgrace. Since they had the map, they probably had very little use for the woman. Oh, they maybe saw *some* use for her, all right.

But as soon as they'd had their fill—if you could ever have your fill of a woman like Paloma Collado—they'd likely shoot her and throw her into an arroyo as wolf bait.

Yeah, that's probably what would happen to her, and why in the hell did it matter to Yakima Henry? He had no dog in this fight. Oh, he'd spent a night with the woman. She'd given him a rollicking good time. One he'd likely remember for years to come. But she was every bit as much of an outlaw as the man she'd poisoned. Every bit as much of a thief.

Yakima didn't need the kind of trouble a stolen army payroll could bring.

So why did he find himself, fifteen minutes later, hard on the trail of Bruno Hilger and Edgar MacElvy?

Because he was as stupid as Paloma had told La Paz he was. That's why. And he couldn't get the bewitching memories of last night out of his head.

He didn't try to overtake the two kidnappers of Paloma Collado. That would be foolish by the light of day, when they could so easily spy him on their backtrail and set up an ambush. Instead, he kept them at the far edge of his vision and followed their trail across the uneven floor of the hot, bristling, rocky desert.

Hell, he told himself by way of rationalizing his actions, they were headed south and, since he was headed south, he might as well trail them and once he caught up to them, he'd see about doing what he could for the girl. He suspected that Hilger and MacElvy were no better than she was, and, since she was a whole lot better looking, he might as well spring her from the trap they'd set for her.

Then what he'd do, he had no idea. No point in thinking that far ahead. He sure as hell wanted nothing to do, however, with a stolen army payroll. He might be wanted by the law, but for unreasonable reasons. He was not an outlaw.

Steadily, doggedly, he followed his quarry across the desert. Up and over low hills, through shaggy, rocky arroyos littered with animal bones and, in one, the strewn half-rotted remains of a human—most likely an Apache, judging by the bits and pieces of calico and deerskin littering the area around the bones. Probably a warrior killed in a skirmish with another tribe or with a cavalry patrol.

The sun dropped behind the western ridges standing in near-black silhouette against the rage of bayoneting pastels. Yakima had slowed his progress when the shadows of dusk had grown long, wary of riding into an ambush, when the distance-muffled crack of a pistol echoed from somewhere ahead of him. Close on its heels came a woman's shrill scream.

Yakima jerked back on Wolf's reins, frowning into the distance. The black wickered uneasily. The half-breed echoed his mount's sentiment with: "Now, what?"

***

Fifteen minutes earlier, the albino, Bruno Hilger, dropped his saddle on the ground near the fire ring that his beefy partner, Edgar MacElvy, had built after gathering wood, and stood threateningly over Paloma Collado. He glared down at her through his weird, colorless eyes set in shallow, pink sockets, brushed a hand across his blunt nose, which he'd smeared with salve against sun blisters, and held out his hand as if to shake hers.

He snapped his fingers.

"Let's have it."

"Have what?"

"What you got from La Paz!"

Paloma glared up at the strange-looking gringo with the long, colorless hair tumbling down over the collar of his blue wool uniform shirt. His pale, faintly freckled cheeks were gaunt and hollow, giving him a cadaverous appearance. His yellow neckerchief buffeted in the finally-cooling breeze that made the flames in the fire ring flutter and smoke.

She removed her sombrero in disgust, tossed it down beside her. "How did you know . . .?"

"That La Paz was with his brother?"

The big man with thick, wavy, light-red hair, a bull neck, and a broad unshaven face with angry eyes was on one knee, snapping twigs and feeding them to the fire. "Hell, I've known for a long time the padre was a half-brother of that old bandito. I always believed him when he told me he rarely saw hide or hair of his darker half. Didn't believe him so much that when the old bandito was known to be in the area . . . and was known to be gravely wounded . . . I didn't pay him a visit.

"Trouble was, when me an' my white-haired friend got to the padre's shack, La Paz was so out of it he couldn't remember his own name, much less where he'd buried the loot. The bandito was only about one-quarter conscious and howlin' like a leg-trapped mountain lion. Likely would be for days . . . if he lived. Nasty mess, them 'Paches make, scalpin' a man, burnin' out one of his eyes with a hot coal."

MacElvy grimaced. "We were in Horsetooth, waitin' around for him to heel up enough to deal."

"To deal?"

"Yes, deal," said the albino. "The location of the loot for his life."

MacElvy said, "Found out it's rather common knowledge around Horsetooth you was meetin' up with the bandit in some old, abandoned casa just outside town." He chuckled. "Is that a blush? You thought it was your secret, huh? Look at that, Hilger, the chiquita's blushin'."

"Looks good on her." Hilger's weird eyes flicked down to her low-cut dress and held there. She'd removed her serape when the day had turned hot. "If only your husband knew what you was sharin' with someone else—a regionally notorious bandito, the very one who'd robbed the army payroll."

Embarrassment burned in Paloma's cheeks. She wondered who in Horsetooth had known about her and Octavio, and how they'd found out. For so long she'd been commending herself on her furtiveness.

She supposed someone, anyone, might have seen her steeling along that goat path to the abandoned casa. It would only take one man, perhaps a boy hunting rabbits in the arroyos, to spy the pretty, young wife of Clancy Brewer out walking alone, and to follow her to her proscribed destination, for the juicy tale to start spreading like wildfire.

Vaguely, Paloma wondered how much longer it would have taken for the indelicate news to have spread to Clancy, who would likely have stripped her naked and whipped her raw with a blacksnake.

"Come on," the albino said, sliding a lock of her black hair behind her ear. "We know he told you where he buried it. We know it's out here somewhere—somewhere in the Chiricahuas, because that's where he was last reported seen with the strongbox. Went into the mountains with it, was ambushed by the patrol sent out from Bryce, and rode out without his hair, his eye, and the strongbox. The one soldier who survived the Apache attack seen him, told about it back at Bryce."

"He didn't tell me about any strongbox,'" Paloma said, feigning incredulity. "I rode out to the padre's shack merely to check on him."

"Bullshit."

"Seriously."

"Seriously, bullshit!" MacElvy laughed. "You know how we know? You was seen out back of Fred's Café in Horsetooth, diggin' up roots. Old Fred Meyer himself said it looked a might suspicious because about the only roots that grew out there was snakeroot . . . and he nor anyone else in town had known you to be such a forager." He winked. "Problem with bein' so damn fun to look at, Miss Paloma, is that most folks in town—at least, most of the *menfolk* in town—keep a pretty watchful eye on ya."

Hilger said, "We doubted we'd ever be able to get the location of the stolen army payroll from La Paz himself. Hell, an old border tough like that can take a lot of pain.

We figured, however, that you could get it out of him, though. And then you'd give him a nice, long drink of that deadly snakeroot. We could tell from the priest's screams . . . and that big happy grin we saw on your face when we first spied you gallopin' along the trail back to Horsetooth . . . that you'd accomplished the nasty task."

Hilger smiled lustily and caressed Paloma's right cheek with the first two, long, pale fingers of his left hand. She jerked her head away from him, revolted, and spit at him. "Go lie with a javelina!" she screeched in Spanish. "A pig is the only one who would couple with such a pink-eyed, vile creature!"

"Oh, I doubt even a pig would lay with ol' Hilger here," laughed MacElvy.

Hilger jerked an indignant look at his partner. "You should talk!" He turned back to Paloma. "Hand it over!"

"Hand what over, fool?"

"He must have written out instructions for locating the strongbox. Or maybe he drew you a map. I know you got somethin'. You looked too happy—and you wouldn't have killed him—to not have got *somethin'*. Hand it over." Hilger stretched his lips back from his yellow teeth grimed with the tobacco he'd chewed and spat with disgusting, liquid plops all the time they'd been riding. "If not, I'd just love to go lookin' for it myself."

His seedy eyes flicked to her bosom.

Again, she recoiled, crossing her arms on her all-but-exposed breasts. "Keep your hands off me, you white-faced devil!"

"That tears it!" Hilger dropped to a knee and, bunching his lips in anger, pushed her back hard against the ground and held her there with one hand around her neck.

Paloma screamed and fought against him as he ran his left hand up the inside of her right leg. He grinned, apparently surprised to discover that she was wearing very little beneath her dress.

Back at the saloon, she'd dressed quickly and skimpily, merely throwing the dress over a pair of silk panties, for she'd wanted to make her trip out to La Paz as quickly as possible. She'd wanted to get back to town before her lover of last night, the handsome, mysterious, green-eyed *mestizo*—Yakima Henry—awakened and lit a shuck out of Horsetooth. She'd wanted to show him the map to the treasure by way of convincing him to help her look for it, as she'd known she'd need a man's help in this dangerous country.

She knew the half-breed to be a very capable hombre in more ways than one.

"Where is it?" Hilger yelled, running his hand brusquely over her writhing body.

"Unhand me, devil!" Paloma shouted, and kicked him hard in the groin.

Hilger yowled, and closed a hand over his crotch. "You little *bitch!*"

"Hilger, knock it off!" yelled MacElvy, who'd just set a pot of coffee on the fire.

Enraged by the assault on his groin, Hilger lunged at Paloma, who tried to skitter back away from him on her rump. He grabbed one of her legs and pulled her back toward him, the dress sliding up around her waist.

"I'm gonna strip you naked and whip the skin right off you, girl!"

MacElvy started to stride over toward his partner and Paloma. One of their horses whinnied shrilly. Both men froze. Hilger twisted around to stare off toward where they'd picketed the horses about thirty yards from the fire.

A gun cracked. Paloma saw the lapping flame in the darkness to the right of the shifting, dark shapes of the horses. She jerked with a start. So did Hilger. Only, the albino wasn't just startled. As he grunted and clapped his hands over his chest, Paloma saw dark, frothy blood geysering out from his breastbone.

"Oh . . . oh, *shit!*" the albino cried, and fell back across Paloma's bare legs.

She couldn't help but scream.

7

There was more shooting and more screaming.

Despite his concern about what was happening in the darkness ahead, Yakima held Wolf down to a fast walk, heading in the direction from which the din of an obvious dustup was originating. There was a little faint green light left in the sky, but only enough to make travel even more treacherous than in solid darkness.

Shadows against faint light could hide dangerous obstacles.

A slope angled up on the half-breed's left. At the bottom of the slope, still to his left and ahead, was a curving wash. He could so no water at the bottom of the arroyo. The gravel paving it was pale in the darkness. Another slope angled up on Yakima's right. He pushed the nervous stallion ahead between the two slopes, but he was moving very slowly now, letting Wolf take only one step at a time.

The sounds of a deadly skirmish had stopped about ten minutes ago. The silence now was denser than before. Two coyotes howled somewhere to the north and there were the distant, infrequent hoots of an owl that seemed to have gotten over whatever anxiety it must have felt over the shooting and screaming.

Yakima had not.

He stopped Wolf amongst some large boulders, dropped the stallion's reins, ground-tying him, and slid his rifle from its scabbard. Pumping a round into the Yellowboy's chamber, he dropped quietly into the wash. He kept his ears attuned to the ratcheting hiss of a sidewinder that might be moving about with more vim and vinegar now that the sun had gone down and the air was cooling.

At the bottom of the wash, Yakima dropped to a knee and doffed his hat so there would be left of his shape to see in the murky, fast-fading twilight. A breeze rustled in the brush to his left, bringing to his nostrils the faint smell of wood smoke. But it was laced with the peppery tang of powder smoke, as well. It was issuing from somewhere ahead of him.

Yakima donned his hat as he straightened and started moving along the bottom of the wash, the four-to-five-foot high banks shifting darkly around to each side of him. There was a sound to his left, and he stopped and dropped again to his knee, holding his breath and pricking his ears.

The sound came again—a man's raspy breath. A boot clipped a stone, sent it rattling.

"Shit!" the man rasped.

He seemed to be moving toward Yakima from down a southern offshoot of the wash that the half-breed was in. Yakima moved quickly forward and to his left, hugging that side of the wash until the mouth of the offshoot appeared only a few yards ahead. The man was still moving toward him, his footsteps growing louder—the thud and crunch of boots on gravel, the faint ching of spur rowels.

All the daylight had faded from the sky, but starlight revealed a man-shaped shadow moving out of the offshoot ahead of Yakima. The man wore a high-crowned black hat. Starlight winked off the barrel of the carbine in the man's hands, and off his spurs. He was a stocky, beefy hombre in a checked shirt, brown leather vest, and denim trousers.

Yakima raised his Yellowboy. "Stop but don't turn around, MacElvy."

The big man jerked with a start but did not turn around.

"Drop that rifle."

MacElvy turned his head to one side. "That you, breed?"

"Drop the rifle."

"Christ!" MacElvy tossed the Winchester carbine into the brush to his left.

"Now the pistol belt."

Looking straight ahead, heavy shoulders rising and falling as he breathed, MacElvy said, "You got it wrong!"

"We'll discuss it when you're lighter by about four pounds, give or take an ounce."

With an air of frustration, cursing under his breath, Edgar MacElvy untied the holster thong from around his stout right thigh, unbuckled the cartridge belt, and tossed the rig into the brush.

"You got anything else?"

MacElvy sighed and lightened his load by a bowie knife and a .41 caliber pocket pistol, both of which he'd slipped out of boot sheaths and also tossed into the brush.

"Turn around," Yakima told him.

MacElvy did, canting his head to one side incredulously. "You just love givin' white men orders, don't ya? You gonna stick your gun up my ass?"

"I got a feelin' you'd enjoy it too much. What the hell was all the shootin' about? Where's the woman?"

"The shootin' was about an ambush I barely evaded. Fortunately, I'm a lot lighter on my feet than I'd appear to be, and I managed to run like hell before they could do to me what they did to Hilger."

"What happened to Hilger?"

"Gone to heaven . . . if he's lucky."

"The woman?"

"Probably wishin' she was with Hilger about now."

Yakima saw a dim umber glow up ahead a ways. "That your fire?"

"Yep."

"Move."

"Mind if I fetch my guns? I—"

"Yes."

Cursing, MacElvy walked on up the arroyo, boots crunching gravel. Yakima followed him up the shallow, left bank and over to where the remains of a fire glowed. A coffee pot hung from a steel tripod over the dull, red coals that were mostly black. The strong smell of scorched coffee tainted the air.

Yakima looked around. The blue-clad Bruno Hilger lay beyond the fire on his back, near a palo verde whose limbs overhung the arroyo. The albino had lost his hat. His ankles were crossed. Starlight shone in his pale, half open eyes. His bloody hands lay palm open at his sides, and his lips were shaped with wonderment.

MacElvy was stumbling around in the brush on the other side of the fire. He cursed under his breath and came out of the brush, saying, "Horse is gone. Either they took him or run him off." He looked at the fire. "Coffee? Probably burned, but it's coffee just the same. You can have Bruno's share."

Yakima turned to face in the direction from which

he'd come, and whistled loudly. MacElvy dropped to a knee beside the fire, lifted the pot with a hook, and swirled it. There was a faint sloshing sound, and seam hissed from spout. "A little left. Probably strong enough to melt a banker's heart, but—"

"Yeah, it's coffee just the same."

MacElvy filled them each a cup and sat down on a rock near his strewn gear. Yakima sat on a log near the arroyo. He could hear Wolf coming at a fast walk.

He blew on the coffee, made a face at the burned leather smell of the scorched brew wafting up with the steam, and said, "Let's start with you tellin' me why you grabbed the former Mrs. Clancy Brewer. Or should I save us time by answerin' my own question? You and Hilger are simply on the sniff for the stolen payroll money as, I assume, are whoever took Paloma out of your incapable hands?"

"Paloma, is it?" MacElvy grinned in the darkness. "Yeah, I suppose last night got you on a first-name basis with the *former* Mrs. Brewer. You sure worked that one fast. Shot her husband then diddled the poor grief-stricken widow seven ways from sundown. Shit, the whole town could hear you two goin' at it. Set the dogs to barkin' and the whores to lookin' all glum."

He laughed.

"Just answer the damn question before I shoot you in the foot, MacElvy."

79

"We figured after the way you two was makin' eyes at each other when me and Bruno left the saloon that she'd draw you into it. Yep, that's what she did, all right."

"How can you be so sure it wasn't love at first sight, you cynical bastard?"

"And, yeah, to answer your question, breed, we took her because we knew she knew where La Paz hid the stolen payroll money. But it ain't what you think."

Yakima sipped the coffee. It was strong, so bitter it made his tongue retreat to the back of his mouth, and bracing.

Wolf climbed the bank and came to a stop behind the half-breed, giving a snort as though to let his rider know he was there, as though his shod hooves couldn't have been heard on so quiet a night from a quarter-mile away. "How ain't it? Were you two aimin' to spread the money around to the poor orphans of Old Mexico?"

"No, our intentions were not quite that noble," MacElvy said. "We were merely going to return it to its rightful owner, the United States government."

Yakima arched a brow. "For the reward?" He chuckled. "Don't try to make me believe you were going to do it simply because you're such good citizens."

"Hilger there's a lieutenant, just like his uniform says, in the U.S Cavalry. Belongs to a special office that investigates payroll robberies out here on the wild frontier.

He's a detective or sorts, I reckon. Or was, more like. Not only that, but he was married to the daughter of the Territorial governor. Can you believe that?"

"Let me work on it."

"And I'm a deputy United States marshal. The head marshal made me throw in with poor dead Bruno there—before he was dead, of course—to investigate the robbery, locate and secure the stolen scrip and specie, return it to Fort Bryce, where it was headed when it was so rudely stolen on its way from Tucson, and bring the dunderheads who stole it to justice."

"I can believe almost anything. You bein' a marshal, MacElvy..." Yakima shook his head. "I can't believe that."

"Believe it. I'll show you my badge, if you promise not to shoot me while I'm reachin' into my back pocket."

"One-handed." Yakima aimed his rifle at Hilger. "Anything else comes out of that pocket besides a badge, you'll be shovelin' coal in hell with Hilger."

MacElvy pulled out a flimsy, brown leather wallet with a badge of a deputy United States marshal pinned inside.

"You could have stolen that," Yakima said, narrowing a shrewd eye.

"Could have."

"All right, I believe you. These is sad times when the federal government is so hard up for badge-toters that they let a fork-tongued, likkered-up old devil like you carry one. Kicked out of the army, no less."

"Takes a special sort to work out here in this dangerous country, breed." MacElvy returned his wallet to his pocket and threw back the last of his coffee. "Now, you gonna let me retrieve my guns? Don't wanna be caught out here unarmed any longer than I have to be."

"How do I know you won't shoot me?"

"I'm a lawman!"

"You're gonna have to better than that, MacElvy."

"All right—how's this? I know you were a scout out here for Fort Hell. A right good one, too. You were green back in them days, but you knew the lay of the land and how to track a man . . . even Apaches . . . across it. Like few others, save maybe the Sergeant, old Gila River Joe." The Sergeant had been Chief of Scouts back at Fort Hildebrandt, or Fort Hell as it was more commonly known, back when Yakima had been on the government payroll. "I need a tracker," MacElvy continued. "I'll pay you two dollars a day out of my own salary, and if we find the stolen payroll, I'll see to it that you're given a reward."

"How much?"

MacElvy spat to one side distastefully. "Five hundred dollars sound about right?"

"How much is in the payroll?"

"Damn near a hundred thousand. Silver certificates, gold and silver coins."

"I'd want at least a thousand for helpin' you retrieve a hundred thousand. Shit, that's only one percent."

MacElvy doffed his hat and ran a hand through his sweaty hair. "All right, goddamnit. Major Fitzgerald—he's the payroll master for the Arizona Division—he's a fair man. If I tell him I promised you one percent, he'll honor it. It is Apache country, after all."

Yakima knew he was giving the Army a hell of a deal, but he didn't need anymore than a thousand dollars. A thousand would get him through the winter all right, over in California, in a little village by the ocean. That's all he wanted. "Who took her?"

"I didn't see 'em. All I know is they were speakin' English without accents, so they weren't La Paz's bunch—the half of the gang he double-crossed after the robbery. Probably just fortune hunters. Plenty enough of 'em out here."

"And common thieves."

"Yay-up." MacElvy waited. "Will you do it?"

Yakima doffed his hat, ran his hand back through his long, black hair. Setting his hat back on his head, he turned to give the unlikely deputy U.S. marshal a level stare. "Up north, I got law trouble."

"Federal or Territorial."

"County sheriff."

"I'll fix it."

Yakima didn't have to think about it. He needed the money, and it would be nice to have that sheriff off his trail. "All right."

"Ha!" MacElvy swiped his hat jubilantly across Yakima's shoulder, almost knocking him off the log he was sitting on. "Thanks, breed. You won't regret it."

"Yeah, right," Yakima said, dryly. It wasn't in his nature to not regret most of his actions. Or, maybe it was just that most of the actions he'd taken over the course of his nearly thirty years had just turned out to be so damned regrettable . . .

What would make him think things were going to change?

"I'm gonna fetch my shootin' irons," MacElvy said ebulliently, and stomped off away from the fire.

"You do that," Yakima grouched.

Behind the half-breed, Wolf reminded his rider of his presence by shoving his long, sleek snout up close to the back of Yakima's neck and giving a deep, uneasy whicker.

"Ah, shut up," Yakima said, and rose to unsaddle the beast. "When I want your advice, I'll ask for it—all right?" He draped a stirrup over his saddle and reached under the horse's belly for the latigo. "And I doubt that time's gonna be comin' anytime soon."

8

Yakima and MacElvy were up before dawn the next morning. They built a fire, and when they'd boiled coffee, the half-breed took a steaming cup of the brew as well as a handful of jerky, and walked a ways out from the camp.

By the gauzy, gray light of dawn, he cut the trail of Paloma's captors.

There were five horses. They'd ridden into Hilger's and MacElvy's camp from the southwest, and they'd left the same way, angling off to the south of the arroyo, in the brush of which quail and cactus wrens were piping.

There was nothing to distinguish any of the tracks—merely five shod horses moving fast across the flat stretch of gravelly, yucca- and greasewood- stippled desert south of the arroyo. Sometimes you'd see that one of the shoes was cracked or had some other flaw in it that would help you track the horse wearing it, but there was nothing like that here.

Judging by the age of some of the horse apples littering the area, the riders had been here awhile before they'd attacked MacElvy and Hilger, and taken the woman. They'd left the horses on a picket line, and five men in run-of-the-mill stockmen's boots had approached the camp on foot. They'd knelt in the dirt, concealed by brush and boulders, which meant they'd either been waiting for the right time to make their move, or they'd been eavesdropping on trio's conversation.

They'd fired from a good distance away. Yakima found their cartridge casings, over a dozen in all, scattered about thirty yards away from the fire.

MacElvy had said they'd just started shooting, and that's when he'd grabbed his rifle and run. The haphazard way they'd gone about their task told the half-breed they hadn't been professionals. Professionals would have gotten closer and shot surer.

Yakima just hoped no others riders obscured their trail. He wanted to catch up to Paloma. He knew it wasn't only because of the job or for the reward money that he wanted to catch up to her. He wanted to catch up to her for some other reason—some instinctive, primitive male reason. A hard, hot knot in the pit of his gut.

She was a killer—that was certain. She'd have killed Yakima for the same reason she'd killed La Paz. But she was a damned ravishing, hypnotic killer, and there was no denying his attraction to her. The frontier was hard on women. Damned hard. Who knew why she'd become what she'd become? He'd like to see that she wasn't tortured or raped, shot or stabbed, and dumped in an arroyo.

She was too much woman for that.

The sun was beginning to separate from the horizon when Yakima started back to the camp. He'd saddled Wolf, and the horse stood ground-tied near the fire that MacElvy had just kicked dirt on. MacElvy tossed away an airtight tin from which he'd been breakfasting, tucked his tin coffee cup into his saddlebags, and picked up his rifle.

"I cut their trail," Yakima said, approaching Wolf. "They're headed toward the mount . . .."

He let his voice trail off as the deputy U.S. marshal loudly cocked his Winchester carbine and aimed the rifle at Yakima. "Sorry, breed. The deal's off. They must've taken my horse; otherwise he'd be back by now. I'll be requiring the use of yours."

"Why, you double-crossin' son of a bitch," Yakima grated out, poking his hat brim back off his forehead.

MacElvy waved his rifle. "Step aside. Get over there by the tree."

"I knew I never should have trusted you."

"I'm truly sorry, breed. I meant to give you the job. Hell, I need a tracker. But I also need a horse. Ridin' double even on your stout stallion there, there's no way we'd get to that payroll strongbox ahead of the others lookin' for it. La Paz's former friends are likely combin' the whole western Chiricahuas about now."

Yakima was exasperated. "So you're just gonna take my horse. That's a hangin' offense—you realize that, don't you, MacElvy?"

"Not in this case. I'm confiscatin' this mount to fulfill my duty as a federal lawman. Like I said, I do apologize." Keeping the cocked carbine aimed at Yakima, MacElvy grabbed Wolf's reins. He winked at the half-breed. "Damn nice stallion, though. I'll be glad to have him."

The lawmen stepped into the saddle. Wolf whickered, shook his head, whickered again.

"Come on, now, don't give me any trouble, black," the lawmen warned.

Off-cocking his carbine's hammer, he rested the barrel across the pommel of Yakima's saddle, and neck-reined the wary horse around. "Good luck, breed!" he called, and ground his spurs into the stallion's flanks.

Wolf whinnied and loped off toward the west, following a well-worn path along the arroyo.

Yakima watched, grinning shrewdly. Then he stuck two fingers between his lips, and whistled. The black whinnied again, louder, stopped, dug his rear hooves into the ground, and lifted his head and front quarters high into the air, catching MacElvy completely by surprise.

The lawman gave an indignant cry as he dropped both his rifle as well as Wolf's reins, and tumbled backward off the mount's rear end. He turned a backward somersault over Wolf's tail and hit the ground with a dusty thud and the crunch and crackle of stiff, abused joints.

"*Oh . . . aah-ohhhh!*" the lawman cried, rolling around in agony while holding his left arm across his belly.

"Serves you right, ya damn fool. Wolf don't like to be ridden by no one else but me, and it don't take much for him to get shed of those he don't want on his back." Yakima grabbed Wolf's reins. "Besides, if you would have looked around, you would have seen your own horse wandered back sometime ago."

He glanced to the north. A brown, bald-faced, blue-eyed gelding stood grazing on the far side of the arroyo, casually cropping wheatgrass. It wore only a hackamore from which its picket rope trailed.

"Shit." Sheepish, his joints crackling, MacElvy climbed to his feet.

***

Yakima didn't take it personally that the pugnacious MacElvy had tried to steal his horse. He knew the belligerent cuss would have done it to anybody. A thousand dollars was a thousand dollars, and he needed that county sheriff off his trail.

They rode together along the trail of the five bush-whackers. Yakima could tell which horse had been carrying both its first rider and Paloma by the slightly deeper indentation of its hooves in the desert sand. The riders had switched the girl to three different horses as they'd ridden between bluffs and mesas toward the southwest and the dark humps of the Chiricahuas.

They'd ridden through open desert, not letting the darkness of the previous night stop them. They'd probably figured that MacElvy, having escaped their drygulching, could be on their trail. Or maybe something else compelled them to ride so hard after dark. Yakima wondered if they'd learned the whereabouts of the loot from Paloma. They seemed to have been making a very purposeful, unwavering beeline for the Chiricahuas, and they'd stopped to rest their horses only twice before Yakima and the lawman nearly rode up on them.

The half-breed heard a sound on the breeze, and then he caught a whiff of woodsmoke.

"Hold up," he told MacElvy, pulling back sharply on Wolf's reins.

MacElvy looked annoyed. "What the hell is it?"

"I think we found 'em."

MacElvy looked around, frowning. "I don't see nothin'."

"Tell you what," Yakima said, swinging down from his stallion's back. "If you learn to use *all* your senses instead of just your eyes, you might, just *might* live to retirement. And quit bein' in such a goddamn hurry. Life's short, MacElvy, and we're dead a long time."

The lawman dismounted with a grunt, the aches from his tumble from Wolf's back still grieving him as his indignation still plucked at him. "Christ, I'm trailin' with a dog-eatin' philosopher. Just my luck."

Yakima swung around, brought a haymaker up from his right hip, and watched the lawman drop like a hundred-pound crate falling from a freight wagon. Both horses sidestepped, whickering. Dust rose around the sprawled MacElvy, who groaned and winced against the dust, and cupped his left hand to his jaw. Blood oozed from an inch-long gash low on his left cheek.

"What the . . . what the *hell* . . . was *that* for?"

"You've eaten as many dogs as I have."

The lawman scowled up at him, working his jaw to check if it was broken. "Don't like bein' called a dog-eater, huh?" He nodded, turning his mouth corners down. "All right. Fair enough."

Yakima slid his 1866 Winchester Yellowboy repeater from its saddle sheath and walked through a crease between high, steep bluffs. As he strode, holding the

Winchester up high across his chest and looking around cautiously, sounds grew in the distance ahead of him. He frowned, trying to place them. It sounded like an Indian's war-whoop. Or the imitation of one. A bad imitation, at that.

Ahead, the buttes leaned back away from him, the crease widening. Beyond lay a small, mud-brick cabin and a barn and two corrals of unpeeled pine poles. Smoke issued from the cabin's stone chimney. A low mesa with boulder-strewn slopes humped behind the place, casting its shadow over most of the yard from which the Apache-like war whoops were originating. Figures milled in the shade, obscured by it. One was moving more than the others.

An arroyo lay between the half-breed and what appeared a small ranch hunkered at the base of the mesa. There was plenty of brush lining both sides of the arroyo, offering cover, so Yakima dropped down into the ravine. As he crossed it, he heard footsteps and low grunts behind him.

He turned to see MacElvy dropping sideways into the wash behind him, boots sliding on the steep cutbank, his spurs rattling faintly. Anger burned between the half-breed's ears. He waved his arm, glaring, and pressed two fingers to his lips. MacElvy caught the look, and his face reddened sheepishly beneath the brim of his high-crowned, black hat.

The big, slope-shouldered lawman took pains to make his tread quieter as he followed Yakima across the arroyo. Wincing, MacElvy sort of hopped on the toes of his worn stockmen's boots. He and Yakima dropped to knees side-by-side, and stared through a thick screen of mesquites and over the beans and fine, slender leaves that had dropped from their branches, toward the small ranch yard.

The raucous howling was coming from a young man hopping Indian-style in a circle before the cabin. A short, lanky kid wearing only a beaded brown vest and black opera hat, with a necklace of what appeared animal teeth flopping across his chest, he was batting his hand against his mouth as he gave his Apache-like, ululating war cry, hopping from one foot to the other.

His schoolyard-style Indian dance rotated around a figure lying spread-eagle on the ground before him. The figure was Paloma Collado. Yakima recognized her without even a stitch of clothes on. In fact, he could probably recognize her better that way.

Her long black hair billowed on the ground around her head, which she lifted frequently to spat and growl and hurl Spanish epithets at the young man dancing around her. As she strained at the four-stakes to which her wrists and ankles were tied, the round, cream globes

of her breasts jostled against her chest. She shook her
head back from her face, and called the kid the off-spring
of a promiscuous weasel.

The kid stopped suddenly and turned to one of the
four other men sitting on the roughhewn front porch of
the cabin, and said, "Pa, can I diddle her? She's awfully
purty! *Can I?*"

9

"Damnit, no, you can't diddle that girl!" raked out a raspy-voiced man sitting back against the cabin's wall, farthest from the other three, all of whom were lounging with either a hip on the rail or sitting on the porch's front step.

They were all staring toward the kid and Paloma.

The man who'd spoke rose and moved to the top of the porch steps, where Yakima could get a better look at him. He was tall and lean, and he wore a suit vest over a hickory shirt, and baggy broadcloth trousers. He wore a bowler hat from beneath which curly gray hair tufted. His face appeared long, angular, and pale save for his nose, which was bright red.

He appeared in his late sixties, early seventies, and he was stooped slightly forward, as though his back had been broken and hadn't healed right.

"We didn't take her for no diddlin'!" he yelled. "She

knows where that payroll money is, and I'll be damned if she won't tell us." The old man glanced at the sky. "Soon as the sun edges over her and starts burning down hot as a smithy's forge, she'll start yammerin' so's we won't be able to shut her up!"

The kid lowered his chin to stare longingly down at her. "I'll shut her up."

"Knute, you get away from there," the old man said, raising his voice until it cracked. "We aren't that kinda people! We don't ravage women!"

No, *Yakima thought*. You just strip 'em and stake 'em out naked.

"Rustlers," MacElvy said out the side of his mouth to Yakima. "Names Vernon Nygaard and his boys. I been wonderin' where they hole up when they ain't rustlin' beef from the ranchers across the southern half of the Territory, doctorin' the brands and sellin' it on the San Carlos Reservation. Vermin. But slippery vermin, for all that. They're killers, all five. That kid's worst of all. He's a cross-eyed little demon, and fast as greased lightnin' with them shootin' irons hangin' off his hips."

Yakima studied the other three sitting on the porch. The one sitting on the top step was whittling, one leg extended, the other leg curled beneath it. A yellow mutt was lying with its head between its paws on the bottom step. The other two men were sitting back against the cabin's adobe brick wall, arms crossed on their chests, staring hungrily toward the girl.

While he studied each man in turn, Yakima was thinking that they must have come upon MacElvy and Hilger's fire the night before, and thought maybe they'd gun the men for their horses and whatever else they had of value . . . including the woman. The old man might have seen himself above rape, but Yakima would have bet silver cartwheels to horse apples he wouldn't see himself above selling her to a top bidder. Out in the loneliest stretches of the territory or down in Mexico, many men would pay as much or even more for a woman than they would for a horse.

Especially as fine a woman as Paloma Collado.

The old man moved down off the porch, the dog getting up and moving away to sit in the yard, also staring toward the girl as though she were a meal it figured it might be indulging in later. Old Nygaard strolled in his bandy-legged way out to where the kid in the top hat stood staring down at Paloma like she was some wonderful toy in a store window.

Nygaard reached into his vest pocket, pulled out what appeared to be wedding cake tobacco and a knife. As he approached the woman, he sliced off a hunk of the wedding cake, and stuck it in his mouth.

"Honey, the sooner you tell us where that payroll

money is, the sooner we'll let you go."

Paloma lifted her head, bent her knees, and spat up at the old man.

"That ain't no way for a purty young woman to act," said Nygaard. "You're only hurtin' yourself, see?"

The other three men—young men of various ages—were coming down off the porch now, grinning. The dogs joined them to sniff around at Paloma's bare feet.

The old man dropped to a haunch beside the girl, holding his open knife over one of her breasts in casual threat.

"The sun's gonna be gettin' right hot. In fact, it's almost here, now." Nygaard glanced at the curved line of sunlight inching toward Paloma. "Save you a lotta time and trouble," he said, working the chaw around in his mouth, moistening it, "if you'd just tell us where it's at."

Paloma told him to go lie down with a horse.

The old man shook his head, scowling, and touched the point of the knife against her breast.

"Ahh!" Paloma said. *"Pig!"*

"How 'bout if I turn you over to my boys?"

"I thought you were not that kind of an hombre!"

"You got me thinking twice about that—surely, you have."

The tallest of the four young men said, "Let me whip her, Pa. I'll fetch a bullwhip from the barn, and whip her good. Then, she'll tell us."

"Get on with ya, Luther," said the young man in the top hat, Knute. "Me . . . I'm gonna diddle the greaser bitch."

"How's that gonna make her do anything but laugh?" asked one of the young men wearing a billowy red neckerchief and holding a sawed-off, double-barreled shotgun in both hands, as though it were a security blanket.

The others laughed. They were standing in a semi-circle around the girl, between her and the cabin. Knute was the only one with his back to the arroyo. Yakima thought that he and MacElvy could probably take them all down relatively quickly, standing as they were, but there was a good chance a bullet would hit Paloma.

Another, larger problem—the dog had stopped sniffing the girl's feet to stare toward where Yakima and the lawman were concealed in the mesquites at the arroyo's bank. The dog was sort of narrowing its eyes and working the black tip of its long, thick, white-mottled, yellow nose, as though it had scented the interlopers.

"Oh, shit . . ." said MacElvy, taking the words out of Yakima's mouth.

"Come on, boys," the old man said, rising. "This girl here is just plain stubborn. Let's let her season out here in the sun for a while and then—"

The young man with the billowy red neckerchief said, "Pa—Rover sees somethin'." He took a long step to one side, tensing and raising his shotgun.

The others stared in the direction at which he was aiming his gut shredder and the dog was staring and sniffing, now whining deep in its throat. The old man had started walking back toward the cabin, but now he turned and shucked both of his Remington revolvers, clicking the hammers back.

"Shit," MacElvy said again.

The dog growled and started trotting toward the arroyo, holding its head down, its eyes dark and suspicious.

"Who's there?" the old man demanded as the rest of his brood stepped away from each other, all drawing at least one weapon. "Show yourselves!"

MacElvy jerked his carbine to his cheek and aimed down the barrel.

Yakima clamped his hand over the carbine's breech. "Hold on!"

MacElvy said, "Hold this!" and jerked his Winchester out of Yakima's grip, and the carbine roared. The dog, ten feet from the arroyo, yipped, wheeled, and ran away, its tail between its legs.

For five seconds, a funereal silence hung over the yard. Yakima turned to stare toward the four men spread out in a semi-circle on the far side of the girl, and toward the kid standing between the arroyo and Paloma. All their eyes were on their father who stood statue-still, extending his pistols straight out in front of him.

Only, now those pistols began to sag. The old man's lips moved as he gasped and took a halting, stumbling step straight backward. He lowered his knobby chin to look down at the red stain growing on the front of his shirt, just left of his heart.

"Dirty bastards," Yakima heard him choke out. "Dirty, rotten bastards killed me, boys . . ."

"You stupid son of a bitch, MacElvy," Yakima said, aiming his Yellowboy repeater as the kid screamed, "Pa!" and the old man sat down as if he'd thought a chair had been behind him.

The others jerked their heads back to the arroyo, and the young man with the red neckerchief cut loose with his shotgun, spraying the ground a few feet in front of MacElvy with buckshot. Yakima drew a bead on the kid, and squeezed the Yellowboy's trigger. The shot sailed wide and thudded into a porch post as the kid, having obviously taken part in lead swaps before, threw himself to his left, and rolled, coming up onto his chest and cutting loose with the shotgun's second barrel.

The buckshot pelted the brush around Yakima and his lawman sidekick, snapping branches and shredding leaves. MacElvy cursed sharply and jerked his head back, wiping a hand across his face as though he'd been bee-stung. Yakima glimpsed smoke and flames lapping from the yard around the now loudly yelling Paloma, and pulled his head down beneath the bank as several bullets plumed dust from the bank's lip.

He crabbed several feet down the arroyo from where he'd been, snaked the Yellowboy up over the bank, picked out a target, and fired. This time he punched a bullet through the billowy red neckerchief, evoking a wild yowl from the kid with the shotgun, who'd tossed the gut-shredder away and was hauling a Schofield out of a shoulder holster.

Yakima managed to drill the thigh of another Nygaard as the tall, lean kid in a striped shirt, suspenders, and armbands fanned a Colt Lightning toward the arroyo.

"*Ach!*" the kid screamed.

He fell, rolled several times, kicking up dust and cursing. He rolled onto his chest and lifted his head, firing another two rounds with his Lightning before Yakima took hasty aim and blew out the kid's right eye, turning the eyeball to instant paste. The kid's head jerked sharply back on his shoulders.

It jerked back again. As it slid forward, there was a hole in the forehead. The head fell abruptly onto its face and the kid lie quivering and rolling his head and shoulders from side to side, as if in vehement denial of his grisly fate.

Yakima glanced to his left. MacElvy had recovered from the barn blaster's pelting and was firing his carbine through the mesquite screen before him. He returned Yakima's glance, blood dripping from several pellet holes in his cheeks and chin and one in his forehead. He gave a sheepish hike of his left shoulder in acknowledgement of the unnecessary shot, and slid his gaze back toward the yard.

He held his fire.

Yakima did, as well.

The half-breed merely stared through his wafting powder smoke, looking for another target. Four of the five Nygaards were down. Only the shotgun kid was moving—writhing, cursing, and spitting blood while clutching his neck as though trying to strangle himself. Yakima drilled a bullet through the kid's forehead, putting him out of his misery though the younker didn't deserve the favor.

Running footsteps and a shrill groan sounded, and Yakima saw the fifth Nygaard, who had long, red hair hanging down from a tan Sonora hat, run out from behind the cabin, limping and casting anxious gazes over his left shoulder. A pistol in his right hand, he ran up the gravelly, red slope at the base of the mesa, disappearing into the formation's shadow.

"There!" MacElvy said, triggering his carbine.

The bullet plumed red dust at the young hardcase's heels as he disappeared into the mesa's dark-purple shadow.

"I got him."

Yakima scrambled up the wash, pushed through the brush, and paused to look down at Paloma, who was smiling up at him, showing all her fine, white teeth between wings of her blue-black hair. "Yakima," she said, brown eyes glinting ethereally in the morning sunshine that was now shining full on the ranch yard. "I knew you would come for me. Somehow, I knew . . ."

The half-breed sighed, dropped to a knee beside her, and couldn't help admiring her fine body, full in all the right places and jiggling to make a man's loins burn, as he slipped his Arkansas toothpick out of its sheath behind his neck and used the five inches of razor-edged Damascus steel to cut her loose.

Free, Paloma sat up and threw herself at him, trying to wrap her arms around his neck. Her breasts brushed against his calico shirt and bear claw necklace before he shoved her aside, rose, stared down at her coldly, and said, "Best get some clothes on before the deputy United States marshal over there starts thinkin' you're a loose woman."

He glanced over at where MacElvy was just then pushing through the brush, growling like a wounded bear and dabbing at his blood-streaked face with a handkerchief. The half-breed didn't wait for Paloma's reaction to hearing the law was present, but jogged along the left side of the cabin and dropped to a knee at its rear corner, aiming his Yellowboy toward the mesa. There was a dark notch in what from a distance had looked like a solid sandstone wall. The fleeing Nygaard must have run into that notch. Yakima threw some lead at the gap, his slugs gouging chunks of sandstone from the wall on either side of it, and then sprinted up the steep, rock-strewn slope, keeping his eyes on the notch in case the kid poked a pistol out of it and started triggering lead.

At the top of the slope, Yakima pressed his right shoulder to the sandstone wall beside the gap, which was a good ten feet wide—a fissure that led into the mesa. He edged a look with one eye into the gap. The corridor between high, sandstone walls was empty. The sky over the corridor was cerulean blue, streaked with high, salmon-green clouds.

The empty corridor was edged in red shadows.

Yakima walked into it, holding his Yellowboy straight out from his right hip, taking one slow step at a time.

Ahead, the corridor curved slightly to the left.

A sound rose from up the notch. It sounded like a gurgling grunt. Then heels and spurs scuffed gravel.

Yakima took two quick steps forward and crouched, tightening his finger on the Winchester's trigger. He held fire. Down the red-shadowy corridor, a man was stumbling toward him. Yakima blinked. At least, it appeared to be a man. Hard to say for sure. It would have helped if the man had had a head on his shoulders. But this hombre had no such thing.

A headless man was stumbling, knock-kneed and heavy-footed, dragging the toes of his boots, toward Yakima. His batwing chaps buffeted around his legs, and the conchos trimming his belt winked in the sunlight angling into the shaft from above. Blood was oozing out the ragged neck, spurting and dripping and bubbling down the front of the man's collarless, pinstriped shirt and butterscotch leather vest.

Yakima crouched, staring, his wide eyes bulging in their sockets. As the headless man's knees buckled, something rose into the air from behind him. Something dark and round. Yakima jerked to the left, and the thing thumped onto the ground just ahead and to his right, between him and the headless corpse that had just now fallen to its knees.

Yakima stared down at the young man's head capped in thick, wavy red hair curling down over the ears. Blood oozed out from the neck, where it had been dislodged from the corpse's shoulders. The face was pale and lightly freckled and there was a half-assed fringe of mustache mantling the upper lip and another fringe of goat beard drooping from the lightly freckled chin.

The pale blue eyes stared up at the half-breed in desperation, the large, black pupils slowly contracting as the eyes blinked once, twice, three, times and then lowered halfway and stopped. The eyes turned instantly to glass.

As the kid's body fell flat on its chest, jerking, an ear-rattling whoop rose behind it.

Yakima stared down the corridor to see the silhouette of an Apache backlit by a broader fissure into which sunlight spilled. Yakima could see the Chiricahua's long hair held back by a red flannel bandanna and the whang strings jostling down the sides of the brave's deerskin leggings. The young warrior jerked his right hand back behind his right ear, and another object came hurling toward Yakima, the wan, reddish light flickering off the wooden handle and feather-trimmed stone head of a war hatchet.

Yakima ducked.

The hatchet turned end over end in the air, whistling, and smashed into the sandstone wall behind the half-breed.

Warm blood had dripped from its head into Yakima's right eye, and he blinked to try to clear it, wincing, as he squeezed the Winchester's trigger. He brushed the blood from his eye with his sleeve, and pumped and fired the Yellowboy three more times, but only watched his bullets hammer dust from the wall where the Indian had been standing.

The brave's whoops and wicked yowls echoed shrilly as they dwindled off down the corridor and into the dense shadows beyond, the taps of his moccasin feet fading to silence.

Heart thudding, Yakima looked down at the headless corpse that was still moving his feet as though trying to run. The eyes in the severed head continued to stare up at Yakima with vague beseeching.

A voice was screaming inside the half-breed's head.

Apaches!

He brushed at the blood on his cheek, turned, and ran.

10

When Yakima had gotten back to the yard, Paloma had pulled on her low-cut cambric dress printed with little yellow suns and moons, and donned her brown sombrero. She was on the ground, her wrists handcuffed behind her back. She was bellowing and throwing her head angrily to and fro as MacElvy sat on her legs, his back facing her, wrapping a rope around her ankles.

"Pig!" Paloma cried, trying to jerk her legs out from beneath the heavy man's weight. "Your mother was the puta pig of all puta pigs! You are feelthy and ugly and you smell *baaaaaddddd!*"

"No point in that!" Yakima said as he ran up to the pair, breathless.

"What do you mean there's no point?" MacElvy said, scowling up at the half-breed. "This little bitch knows where the payroll's at, and I'm not lettin' her out of my sight!" He looked down to knot the rope around Paloma's black, hand-tooled stockmen's boots, into the tops of which a bucking horse had been stitched in white thread. "You get that last Nygaard son of a bitch?"

"Nah, turned out I didn't have to."

MacElvy looked at Yakima again, who was glancing warily back in the direction from which he'd run. "Didn't *have* to?"

"An Apache did the dirty work for me. And believe me, it was dirty. Believe I'll be seein' those two eyes blinkin' up at me for a while, just as soon as I lay my head down on my saddle to go to sleep. We'd best pull our picket pins." Yakima stepped forward and, facing the arroyo, stuck two fingers in his mouth, and whistled for Wolf.

MacElvy had the Southwesterner's understandably exaggerated reaction to the word "Apache."

He stood and faced Yakima, scowling, the nubs of his cheeks turning pale as though with frostbite though the sun was hammering down hot and hard on the dusty ranch yard. "What the *hell* are you talkin' about? You fall on your head?"

"Cut her loose," Yakima said, gesturing at Paloma's tied ankles. "She's gonna have to ride." He headed over to the corral in which the rustling family's horses were running in anxious circles, red dust rising thickly.

MacElvy didn't seem to understand—or to want to

understand. "Cut her loose?"

"Cut her loose!"

By the time Yakima had roped and rigged a buckskin from the rustlers' string of no-doubt stolen horses, and led it out into the yard by its bridle reins, Wolf was pushing up the arroyo bank and bulling through the brush, the lawman's horse hard on the black's heels, both mounts trailing their reins around the ground.

Yakima glanced toward the mesa, relieved to see no sign of Apaches heading toward them. Yet.

He'd only seen one. But Apaches were like rattlesnakes. When you saw one, you could bet the seed bull there was a whole nest of more somewhere close.

MacElvy had cut Paloma's ankles free and removed her cuffs. As he strode over to his horse, Yakima turned to Paloma, who stared up at him with a pouting look of grave injury. "Why did you have to go and bring a *lawman*, of all people? The treasure could be ours, Yakima!"

"Where is it?"

"Where is what?"

"The treasure!"

"You think I'll tell you now . . . after you brought *him?*"

Yakima glanced back toward the mesa. Still no Apaches. He had no doubt they'd be coming soon, however. Those who hadn't allowed themselves to be herded like cattle onto reservations were the wildest of the lot, and they tended to kill white men . . . and women . . . for sport.

There was no time to argue with the woman. He pulled her to her feet and lifted her onto the waiting buckskin. She cursed him and spit at him. Ignoring her, taking the buckskin's reins, he mounted Wolf. MacElvy rode up beside Yakima and grabbed the buckskin's reins out of his hand.

"I'll take those," he said, customarily belligerent. "Don't want you and her gettin' no ideas. You might decide to go dig that money up, just the two of you, and run off to Mexico and get hitched!"

"You smell bad, gringo lawman!" Paloma shouted, red-faced with fury.

"She's got you there, MacElvy," Yakima said with a wry chuckle and putting the steel to Wolf's flanks.

He and the horse bounded through brush and into the ravine. He wasn't sure which way to head but as directly away from where he'd seen the Apache seemed the most sensible route, since he'd seen no sign of the others yet.

He followed the ravine on an angling course west for probably a mile, and then followed a game trail up out of the arroyo and headed south across the desert, the cholla, ocotillo, and occasional saguaros and palo verde trees standing tall around him, obscuring his view in every direction.

The Chiricahua Range stretched from left to right ahead of him, the left end closer than the right end. They were closer now, and their craggy peaks were velvety green with evergreen forests. The land before and around them was a rugged jumble of up thrust rock, strewn boulders as large as cabins, and tabletop mesas large enough to hold a city the size of Denver.

Vast country. All Apache country. Chiricahua country. If he wasn't careful, he was liable to ride away from one group of broom-tailed, bronco warriors into another group. If he had any brains, he'd angle around the mountains and make a beeline for the border, leave MacElvy and Paloma to their own devices.

For some reason, he just couldn't do it. It wasn't just that he was woman-drunk. Seeing that Apache and the headless Nygaard boy had slapped him sober right quick. Now, he felt he was in too deep to just ride away. He'd started something, and he needed to ride it out—whatever *it* was.

He led MacElvy and Paloma to the top of a short, flat-topped bluff and halfway down the other side, to where a spring oozed water amongst rocks sheathed in sand grass and oak shrubs. They were climbing higher now, and the creosote brush was giving way to sagebrush, gooseberry, and wild rose. They weren't high enough to escape the stifling heat, however.

Yakima remembered this spring from the time, a couple of years ago, when he and his now-dead wife, Faith, had ridden here from their little ranch on the slopes of Mount Bailey to trap wild horses in the deep canyons flanking the Chiricahuas. Most southwesterners had a good memory for water, drawing clear maps in their minds.

Faith...

No, he wasn't going to start thinking about her now.

"I want some water!" Paloma said.

MacElvy glared at her. "Why don't you just talk a little louder so you'll bring them 'Paches right down on top of us?"

Paloma slipped down from her saddle and leaned far forward, flaring her nostrils at MacElvy. "You smeeellll baaaaad, lawman."

Yakima slipped his spyglass in its little hide pouch from his saddlebags, and walked back up the slope. Near the top of the bluff, he got down on his knees, doffed his hat, and raised the glass to his right eye, shielding the lens with his right hand to keep it from flashing in the sunlight.

He scanned the dun-colored corduroy country tufted with lime-green behind them, marked here and there with snaking, cream-colored watercourses and interrupted by hulking sandstone or black volcanic dykes or mesa formations. He was looking for mares' tails of rising dust, but after he'd scanned the country for nearly five minutes, he saw nothing.

That didn't make him feel any better about their situation. When there was one Apache, there were always more, and he had to assume they were following him, because that was the only way you stayed on your toes and kept your head in *Apacheria.*

"Anything?" MacElvy said, just loudly enough for Yakima to hear. The lawman was sitting on a rock near the spring, keeping his rifle aimed at Paloma, who was sitting back and combing spring water through her hair with her fingers. Her sombrero was hooked over one upraised knee.

Yakima reduced the spyglass, donned his hat, and moved back down the slope. "Nothin'."

"You sure you saw an Apache?"

"Yeah, I've seen 'em before. I know what they look like."

"Don't get your dander up, breed. Uh . . . ." MacElvy grinned sheepishly. His face was streaked with dried blood from the half-dozen shotgun pellets he'd taken, and the little wounds were swelling. "I mean . . . Yakima. It's just that I ain't seen any on our trail since we left the rustlers' ranch, and, believe me, I been keepin' an eye out for 'em."

"They're back there, all right." Filling his hat at the spring, Yakima glanced at Paloma, who was cool toward him now, unwilling to meet his gaze. He said, "Enough screwin' around. Where's that payroll loot?"

She cursed him mildly in Spanish, smiling at him winningly.

Yakima set his water-filled hat down in front of Wolf. He scratched the back of his head, and said, "Wait a minute—he scribbled you a map. Yeah, I remember, he scribbled you out a map to the loot, La Paz did."

"No shit?" said MacElvy.

"You are both fools," Paloma said. "Do you think I have it on me?" She raised her hands. "I memorized it, tore it up, and tossed it to the wind."

"I don't think you had time to memorize it," Yakima said. "Where is it?"

"Hell, they had her staked out on the ground naked as a jaybird but a whole lot better lookin'," said MacElvy, narrowing a lusty eye at the woman. "If anyone would have found it, they would have found it."

"Did you like what you saw, old man?" Paloma asked him in that insouciant tone of hers.

"Yeah, I liked it just fine," MacElvy said. "I bet the breed here . . . uh, I mean *Yakima* here . . . liked it even better . . . back at your husband's hotel."

"I assure you he did," Paloma said.

Thumbs hooked in his pocket, one hip cocked, Yakima studied her comely figured barely concealed by the thin, dusty dress that hung low on her shoulders. "The Nygaards wouldn't have known to look for a map."

He stepped toward Paloma who crossed her arms on her breasts. "Leave me alone. I told you—I don't have the map. I tore it up and . . ."

"I know, threw it to the wind." Yakima knelt beside her and lifted her skirt high up and away from her left leg. "I think you're a liar. I think you still got it on you . . . where?"

"Stop!" she insisted, tugging at the dress.

Yakima lifted her dress up her legs, inspecting the hem. He brusquely rolled her onto her belly, holding the skirt up high. She wasn't wearing a stitch of underwear except a thin pair of silk panties. The panties weren't large enough to house a map—they were so insubstantial, in fact, that he could have wadded them up in his mouth and still have had room to chew a full meal—but she might have an inside pocket in her dress . . .

Paloma cursed him and punched and kicked her black boots at Yakima, who, ignoring the pummeling, thoroughly inspected the dress and the woman's naked body underneath it. MacElvy howled. When he'd given the dress a good going over, the half-breed left her cursing belly down on the ground, dust wafting around her, and grabbed her hat.

She reached for the sombrero. "Pig, give me that!"

Yakima pulled it away from her, and rose. He looked inside the low-crowned sombrero. Inside the brim was a thin, leather pocket. He slipped his index finger and thumb into the pocket and pulled out a neatly folded scrap of notepaper.

"You are the child of a whore!" Paloma spat out at him, rising, her dress hanging down off one arm and revealing nearly all of her beautiful left breast. "Give me that! It is no business of yours! It is between me and La Paz!"

MacElvy grabbed her around the waist and, laughing, spun her around. "You're a foxy little thing, Miss Paloma!"

While the lawman held the raging woman, Yakima inspected the map hastily drawn in pencil. It had been drawn for someone who knew the country, for it wasn't very detailed. There was one detail that caught the half-breed's eye, however. He didn't recognize it right away, but when he realized what the mark signified in relation to the other marks around it, he lowered the map and scowled off to the southwest.

Toward where a broad shoulder of the Chiricahuas humped darkly, broodingly against the brassy sky, striped with cloud shadows.

"Ah, shit."

"What is it?" MacElvy said.

Paloma suddenly grew silent in defeat. She stared at Yakima, hard-eyed, jaws like stone, the hot breeze sliding her hair around her shoulders.

"Why?" Yakima said, staring into the southwestern distance. "Of all the goddamn places in the Chiricahuas he could have hid that loot, why in hell did he have to hide it *there?*"

11

"So . . . where'd he hide it? What's on the damn map?"

MacElvy sounded a little reluctant to ask the question. Now it came, an hour after Yakima had voiced his dismay at the loot's location.

They'd ridden up into cooler, fresher country—pine country. Lodgepoles and firs towered around them, silhouetted against the bright sunlight pouring like liquid brass through the canopy in which squirrels chittered, blackbirds cawed, and nuthatches and chickadees peeped.

The tang of pine resin was so strong it nearly took the half-breed's breath away at times.

Yakima was riding at the head of the three-person line, Paloma riding behind him, MacElvy bringing up the rear, holding his carbine butt up on his right thigh.

"It's an old stone line shack beside a pretty creek bubbling down out of the higher reaches. A damn pretty place."

MacElvy said with gentle probing, "I take it you been there before?"

"Yep."

They continued riding along at a moderately slow, even pace, climbing a long, gentle grade through the pine forest, occasional basalt escarpments humping up around them. High overhead, a hawk was hunting, giving its ratcheting screech. Sometimes pinecones tumbled to the forest floor with quiet thuds, and the breeze rustled the boughs, the cool air drying the sweat on Yakima's face.

"This ain't a place you care to go back to," MacElvy said after a while, with the same halting prodding as before.

Yakima pulled back on Wolf's reins, curveted the horse, and glared back at the broad-shouldered, round-bellied lawman riding up from about forty yards away, beyond Paloma on her buckskin. Both the other two riders stopped when they saw the hard look in the half-breed's eyes.

"Let's just leave it at that, MacElvy."

The lawman studied him for a time. So did Paloma.

Finally, MacElvy rolled a rounded shoulder, smiled, and said, "Okay. All right. Just curious, is all."

"Yakima." Paloma pulled the buckskin up to within ten feet of the half-breed. Her eyes were round and soft. She hadn't called him anything but a pig since he'd rescued her from the rustlers' ranch, so this was a change. "You know there is almost a hundred thousand dollars in gold, silver, and paper money in that box."

"That's what I hear."

"If you shoot this man, this so-called *lawman*, it can all be ours."

"Hey, now," MacElvy objected.

"He is not even a lawman," Paloma said, wrinkling her nose at him. "He calls himself one, but everyone knows he is an outlaw. He stole that badge from the deputy United States marshal he killed. Everyone knows that, too, but no one says anything because they are afraid of him. He runs with no gang, but he is a killer. A shootist. A regulator. If someone wants somebody dead, and they have enough money to hire it done, they hire him to do it."

"Well, now, listen to this," MacElvy said, laughing. "That's pretty damn good. You must've been concocting that story for a time now. That's why you been so damn quiet. Been runnin' your brain instead of your mouth for a change. That lie ran pure as rain water off your devilish little tongue, senorita."

MacElvy caught Yakima studying him, and he opened and closed his gloved hand around the breech of his carbine.

"Don't make the mistake of falling for that, now, bre . . . uh, Yakima. She's pretty, and I'm sure you had a good time in the sack with the lyin' little trollop, but lyin' little trollop is just exactly what she is."

Paloma stared at Yakima, her wide, dark-brown eyes deep with desperation. "Once he gets his hands on that money, he's going to kill you. And then he'll kill me"—she turned to stare in repugnance at the beefy lawman—"after he's done what he's been imagining doing to me, that is." She shuddered. "The thought sickens me. I'd rather lie with *javelinas*."

Yakima said, "That how it is, MacElvy? She's right— you could have taken that badge off any old dead lawman's corpse. There's probably more dead lawmen in these parts than livin' ones."

MacElvy pointed with the hand holding his reins. "Don't you fall for it, breed. She'd like nothin' more than to get you an' me crossways!"

"Maybe we're already crossways," Yakima said. "And I just don't know it."

MacElvy booted his horse up slowly toward the half-breed. He glowered at the girl and turned back to Yakima. "She's a liar. Plain and simple. Remember how she poisoned her beloved Octavio?"

"You are the liar," Paloma said in a hard, quiet voice. "You are a lying pig. Yakima, I swear on my mother's grave . . . on the grave of—"

"Octavio's grave?" said MacElvy, laughing.

"Shut up, pig! I swear on the grave of *mi padre*. He is

lying. Sure as we are sitting here now, he will shoot us both as soon as he gets his hands on that strongbox."

MacElvy's face turned the red of Arizona sandstone as he jutted his jaws at Paloma. "You know what I'm going to do to you, you little—?"

"All right, all right," Yakima said. "This is gettin' us nowhere. Let's get on up to the shack before the sun goes down. We got another hour of easy ridin' left. MacElvy, I'd appreciate it if you rode up here next to me instead of behind me, like you been doin'."

"Ah, shit," the lawman complained, shaking his head and glaring at the woman.

Paloma curled one side of her upper lip, pleased with herself.

"All right, all right—we'll ride together," MacElvy said, putting his dun up beside Yakima. "But she rides ahead, then, where I can keep an eye on her. She's under arrest."

"For what?" Yakima asked. "She hasn't done anything yet except poison a known outlaw."

"I'll think of somethin'."

"You smell baaad, outlaw," Paloma said, leaning forward in her saddle and slitting her eyes maliciously.

"And that's enough out of you about how he smells," Yakima reprimanded her. "I think we can all agree he doesn't smell like no poppy field in May, but I'm tired of hearin' about it. In fact, I'm tired of this whole damn thing."

MacElvy extended his gloved hand. "Why don't you just give me the map and ride away, then? We're close enough now I can find it on my own. And if there were any Apaches on our trail, we'd have seen 'em by now."

"Ha!" Paloma said. "I'd be feeding the cougars by sunset!"

MacElvy slitted one eye at Yakima. "You know, if it makes you feel any better, I can't trust you anymore than you can trust me. She's made you one right enticin' offer. Her and a hundred thousand dollars. Boy, you two could have a right wonderful time with all that loot! Why, you could move to San Francisco and buy you a big fancy house, lounge around in silk pajamas, and never have to work another day in your life."

"I know—it does sound good," Yakima said, rubbing his chin. "I've never had me no silk pajamas. Let's get movin'. Paloma, get up there. And, you, MacElvy, I'd just as soon you stowed that carbine in your saddleboot. If you haul it out for no good reason that I can see, you're gonna look mighty funny with it sticking out your hind end."

MacElvy slid the Winchester into the saddleboot. "You got a thing about stickin' firearms up men's asses."

Yakima winked. "I do, at that."

As the three started off once more, moving through the pine-fragrant, sun-dappled forest, the beefy lawmen spat, sighed, and shook his head. "Now, this is a shame. You've gone and let this little Mexican trollop sour what I was startin' to think was a nice little partnership." He spat. "Damn shame."

***

Around an hour later, they rode up into a little clearing on the shoulder of a mountain that overlooked the vast, dun stretch of the desert from which they'd just come. It was rocky here, and the rocks seemed to sprout pine and fir trees. This was on the mountain's western edge, and the angling sun stretched long tree and escarpment shadows, so that the hovel was almost hidden in a niche in the rocks and trees.

An eagle was perched on the house's steeply pitched roof thatched with pine boughs. There were no shutters over the windows, and no door, and the cavities stared out on the clearing like the empty eye sockets of a bleached skull. The eagle watched the three riders draw near—the two men riding side by side, following the woman.

When the group was fifty yards from the shack, the eagle spread its large ungainly wings, launched itself with its black-taloned feet, and made a creaking, whooshing sound as it flew up and over the interlopers. The wind ruffling its brown feathers, it gave an indignant screech as it topped the pines with a whoosh and disappeared against the dark-green of the late afternoon sky arching like a vast bowl over the craggy peaks of the Chiricahuas.

Yakima reined Wolf up in front of the shack. He pushed away the memories that threatened to wrap themselves around him like slithering snakes, and instead inspected the shack objectively, making sure no one else was here.

Hearing and seeing nothing but blackbirds cawing in the pine boughs, he turned to MacElvy regarding him expectantly. The man said nothing. He stretched an eager half-smile, and arched a brow. Paloma dismounted and stood holding her buckskin's reins, an oblique look in her dark eyes.

Yakima swung down from Wolf's back, dropped the reins, and fished the hastily scrawled map out of his pocket, wrinkling his brows as he inspected it. He grimaced, gave the scrap of notepaper to the wind, which sent it sailing off across the gravelly, rocky ground toward the tan desert stretching off to the west.

"Map just indicates the cabin," he said, looking around. "Doesn't say exactly where La Paz stowed the loot." He doffed his hat, ran his elbow around the sweatband, soaking the sweat up with his shirtsleeve, then stuffed the hat back on his head. "Let's take a look around."

MacElvy and Paloma silently dogging his steps, he inspected the inside of the shack. Save for pine needles and cones and windblown leaves and a couple of packrat nests and spider webs, the three-room shack was as empty as a cave. He brushed past the lawman and Paloma and went out to stand just outside the shack's door, on the sunken, badly worn patch of ground fronting it.

He'd figured the place had been a line shack for some old *hacendado* who'd run a *hacienda* in the area and maybe still did. When he and Faith had spent time up here, corralling wild horses to take back to their ranch on the slopes of Mount Bailey farther north, he'd imagined the old vaqueros who'd taken up residence here from time to time, and all the Mexican tobacco they'd no doubt smoked, wearing away the ground in front of the door.

Then he remembered . . .

His face brightening speculatively, he swung to his right.

"Hey, where you goin'?" MacElvy asked suspiciously behind him.

Yakima walked around the north side of the shack to the back. MacElvy and Paloma followed him, MacElvy striding quickly, scowling. Yakima dropped to a knee at the back wall of the shack, and studied the ground. Slowly, he smiled.

"It's here, all right."

"Where?"

Yakima used his gloved right hand to smooth away

the thin skin of dirt and pine needles that had been tossed a little too carefully over the area, to reveal several halved pine logs.

"I left these exposed," he said, "last time I was here. Other pilgrims probably used this hole for the same thing we did."

"Root cellar?" asked MacElvy.

"Of sorts."

"Well, let's have a look at it."

The lawman jerked his trousers up his broad thighs, and knelt with a grunt on the opposite side of the halved logs from Yakima. The logs were about four feet long. Both men pried them up with their fingers, and tossed them aside. They stared down into the four-feet-deep hole that was roughly four feet square.

Neither said anything. They just stared down at the wooden box banded with rusty steel and lightly dusted with dirt and pine needles. There was a padlock on the hasp but the lock was open. There were two ragged-edged bullet holes through the front of the lock.

Obviously, the box hadn't been in the hole for more than a few weeks.

"Well, it ain't gonna just come floatin' up out of there on its own," MacElvy said, grunting as he lowered his right arm into the hole. "Help me, here!"

"Hold on." Yakima was staring into the breeze-brushed

pines and pale rocks and boulders beyond the shack's rear, up along a storybook stream that trickled down the mountain to jog a curving course along its base.

MacElvy turned to follow his gaze. "What is it?"

A fir bough moved. To the left of that bough, a pine-cone dropped from another one, landed with a soft thud on the slight incline, and rolled several feet to plop into a small, dark bend in the stream.

"Thought I heard somethin'."

"What?"

Slowly, Yakima rose, staring into the trees and rocks near the trickling water, and unsnapped the keeper thong from over the hammer of his holstered Colt. He wished he had his Yellowboy, but he'd left it on his horse. He glanced at Paloma who stood just off the corner of the shack, staring into the forest, her eyes apprehensive, the breeze tussling her hair and nipping at her dress.

Yakima drew his Colt and walked over to the edge of the trees, staring up the incline amongst the trees and escarpments, the tang of pine and warm forest duff heavy in his nose. He saw nothing but the trees and the moving branches, a squirrel flicking its upraised tail as it scolded him from a juniper farther up the slope.

"I don't see nothin'," said MacElvy, who'd come up to stand beside him, the lawman holding his own Rem-ington .44 down low by his right thigh. "But now you got me wonderin' about Apaches. Sure wouldn't want to get caught in this clearing with twenty, thirty of 'em movin' around us."

Yakima stared up the slope for another minute.

"Musta been my imagination," he said, returning the Colt to its holster.

"Seein' one Apache will make you see more even when there ain't more to be seen. Come on—let's get that box up outta that hole!"

"Yeah," Yakima said, reluctantly giving his back to the slope and following the lawman back toward the strongbox. "I reckon."

12

Yakima took one end of the box and MacElvy took the other end, and they pulled it up out of the hole, cursing and grunting with the effort. The lawman turned the box toward him, his eyes so wide that Yakima thought they'd pop out of their sockets, and removed the padlock from the hasp. He opened the creaky lid.

"Hol-leee . . .!"

Yakima glanced around the side of the box to see inside. There were wads of greenbacks and canvas pouches that no doubt contained gold and silver.

MacElvy laughed and pulled out one of the packets of scrip with one hand, a coin pouch with the other hand. He hefted both. The coins rattled. "Damn near one hundred thousand dollars!"

"You could go a long way on that much money, Marshal." Yakima glanced at Paloma who, inexplicably, had not reacted to the finding of the strongbox or the money inside it. In fact, now she merely turned and walked back around toward the front of the shack.

Yakima turned back to MacElvy and said, "That is what you are, right, MacElvy?" After all they'd been through to locate the strongbox, he wanted the reward money he'd been promised. He'd be damned if he was going to let the lawman—if that's what he really was—abscond with the goods. He would let himself be taken for no fool. When a woman did—that was one thing. But he didn't want a man doing it.

MacElvy looked at Yakima from beneath his bushy brows, and pursed his lips. "Ah, that's a shame—you believin' that girl's lies. Just a shame. Of course I'm a lawman, and I'll be headin' out first thing in the mornin'—takin' it back to Fort Bryce."

"*We'll* be headin' back to Bryce," Yakima corrected him.

MacElvy was putting the money back into the strongbox. "Yeah, yeah—I meant 'we.' Of course, that's what I meant. Take an end, will ya?"

They carried the box back around to the front of the shack. They set the box down by the front door, the lawman saying, "I reckon here's a good a place to stow it as any. We'll bivouac right here in the front yard, where we can both keep an eye on it." He chuckled.

"Sounds right by me . . . Marshal," Yakima said, giving

the man another suspicious look. MacElvy had seemed a little too pleased about finding all that dinero. *Outlaw*-pleased as opposed to *lawman*-pleased.

MacElvy looked at him, breathing hard from exertion, and mopped his neckerchief across his face pocked and swollen from the opera-hatted kid's buckshot. "Shame," he said, wagging his head sadly again. "Damn shame." He frowned as he looked out across the clearing. Paloma was walking out there, heading toward an escarpment at the edge of the mountain that offered a view of the desert below, out beyond the foothills. "Look there," he said. "Looks awful sad, don't she?"

She did look sad, Yakima thought. He supposed he'd feel sad, too, if he went to all the work she'd gone to for a hundred thousand dollars and gotten it swiped out from under her. He didn't feel too badly for her, though. She'd done nothing to give MacElvy cause to arrest her, so she was a free woman. A free *poor, widowed* woman, but a free woman, just the same.

A haunted feeling came over him again, and he moved to a corner of the shack, staring up the slope he'd felt compelled to investigate a few minutes ago. Hair bristled at the back of his neck—an old, cautionary sensation, one he'd done well to heed in the past. He had a feeling the Apaches had followed them, after all.

Why they didn't strike, he didn't know. Maybe they

were waiting till sundown though most Apaches in general did not like to wage war at night.

But maybe they thought that taking down only two men and one woman wouldn't really be much of a war.

Damn funny, though, that they hadn't shown themselves by now.

Maybe MacElvy had been right. Maybe seeing that one Apache had caused the half-breed to have Apaches on the brain. He'd be damned, though, if he didn't feel someone watching from the forest.

He went back and stripped his gear off Wolf. He had an urge to get the hell out of that little clearing, but the sun would be down in an hour and the cabin, even without shutters over the windows, would probably offer as much protection as anyplace else.

He'd sleep outside where he could keep an eye on things.

He tossed his gear down in front of the cabin. He stripped the gear off Paloma's mount, as well, and tossed it down near his and MacElvy's. He fed and watered Wolf and then gave the horse a thorough rubdown with a scrap of burlap. MacElvy was doing the same to his brown gelding, looking mighty pleased with himself over the loot. That made the half-breed uneasy. The lawman just looked too damn pleased, as though he had every intention of keeping the money for himself.

PETER BRANDVOLD

When he'd inspected all of Wolf's hooves, pulling a couple of cactus thorns out of the frogs, Yakima picketed the mount on a rope line that MacElvy had strung between two gnarled cedars, near a pool in the stream that ran down the mountain.

Then he tramped off to join the lawman in collecting firewood.

As he did, he kept looking around for suspicious movement around the canyon that was growing darker and darker, and quieter and quieter. From time to time he looked off to where Paloma sat in the rocks overlooking the desert, which was pink and salmon now as the sun tumbled behind the Dragoons in the northwest, its long shadows growing.

She looked so glum about losing the strongbox that Yakima almost felt sorry for her. At the same time, he knew she'd just as easily have poisoned him as La Paz, if he'd been in La Paz's position. Drinking snakeroot was about the same as drinking lye—a hard way to die. Not that he felt much sympathy for La Paz, however.

When it was nearly dark, she came over to the camp and accepted a cup of coffee from Yakima. MacElvy was in a celebratory mood. While they boiled a pot of beans to which Yakima had added the jerky remaining in his food pouch, the lawmen shared his whiskey with his campmates, adding a splash to the coffee of each.

Yakima ate a bowl of beans and sipped the coffee laced with bourbon and tried not to let the fire compromise his night vision, as he wanted to keep his eyes skinned for possible Apaches steeling down from the surrounding ridges. Or for whoever may be on the lurk up there.

"How 'bout a game of cards?" MacElvy asked after they'd all eaten and cleaned their plates at the stream, and Yakima had checked the horses.

Paloma shook her head and rolled up in her blankets, turning onto her side and resting her head against the underside of her saddle.

"Yakima?" MacElvy asked.

"Nah, think I'll get a little shut-eye," the half-breed said, pulling his hat brim down over his eyes as he too reclined against his saddle.

MacElvy chuckled as, lying on one hip on his blanket roll, he began laying out a game of solitaire. "Shit, you ain't gonna sleep a wink."

"How's that?"

"You got your neck up over me and 'Paches. Me—I ain't worried. If 'Paches were near, that horse of mine would be goin' wild. He'd pull them cedars he's tied to plum out of the ground!"

Yakima glanced at where both horses lay in black humps beyond the cabin and near the base of the ridge, where the little stream curved. MacElvy had a point. Wolf would be kicking up a Texas-sized twister, too, if he so much as whiffed an Apache, and he could wind an Apache from a quarter mile away.

"All right," Yakima said, pulling his hat brim down over his eyes for a second time. "Maybe I'll catch my forty winks, after all, MacElvy. Thanks for putting my mind to rest."

"Shit, you still ain't gonna sleep."

Yakima grunted in frustration, and poked his hat back up off his forehead again. "Somethin' on your mind?"

The lawman snapped a pasteboard down onto another card and grinned with one side of his mouth, the firelight playing over his broad, shot-pocked face in need of a shave. In the guttering firelight, the pores in his skin as well as the swollen pellet wounds looked large and dark, giving him a menacing aspect. The hollows of his eyes were also dark though the eyes themselves were tiny red dots beneath his hat brim.

"You're gonna be worried I'll gun you in the night and run off with the loot." He chuckled and shook his head. "Shit, you ain't gonna sleep a wink."

Yakima turned up his left cheek with a burn of annoyance. The former-sergeant-turned-lawman hadn't changed one stripe over the years. He was still as much fun to have around as a hydrophobic boar hog. "Yeah, well, you're gonna be thinkin' the same thing about me, so don't get all high-hatted about it."

MacElvy's dark nostrils flared, the orange firelight playing over his big nose. "Yeah . . . well . . . keep in mind, even if I should nod off, I'm a light sleeper. And I can *smell* a man aimin' a gun at me!" He turned his head slightly toward where Paloma lay soundlessly beneath her blankets, her back to the fire. "Women."

***

MacElvy had been right. Yakima couldn't sleep despite being sleepy. He'd nod off and just begin to feel the warm, soothing arms of slumber wrap around him before an image floated up through that murky warmth. It was MacElvy's devil face, eyes flashing wickedly, grinning, as he raised his cocked Remington.

Then Yakima would jerk his head up with a grunt, reaching for his own pistol and shooting a fearful look across the umber coals of the near-dead fire toward where MacElvy lay mounded inside his own soogan.

MacElvy had been right about Yakima's sleepless night. But Yakima had been wrong about MacElvy's. The big, pugnacious lawman seemed to be sleeping just fine, his chin rising and falling as he snored luxuriously, making raspy whistling sounds with each exhalation.

"Son of a bitch," Yakima muttered, and tossed his

blanket back.

He rose to his knees and cast a glance toward where both horses still lay as before, sound asleep. Obviously, there were no Apaches in the area.

That was good. But Yakima felt an almost undeniable urge to trigger his pistol into the air and give MacElvy something to think about. The only reason he didn't was because he didn't want to wake Paloma. No need for that.

He heaved himself to his feet, pulled on his moccasins, wrapped his Colt and shell belt around his waist, and stomped off into the clearing beyond the cabin. There was no moon but there were so many stars that the clearing seemed to glow as though from a pearl light emanating from the ground. He could see every sage clump and hackberry shrub.

A lone owl hooted somewhere on the ridge to his right. Far off across the dark desert stretching away to the west, a couple of coyotes were holding a wild conversation though it was barely a murmur up here on this stony mountain shoulder.

He climbed to a perch in the rocks overlooking the desert that was a soft tan in the darkness below and beyond. When he'd waggled his big body into a comfortable position against the rough escarpment wall behind him, he dug his makings sack from his shirt pocket. He paused, weighing the sack in his hand. Might be foolish smoking out here, but if there were Apaches around, he'd likely know by now.

Damn stupid, him getting hooked on tobacco. He'd gotten started smoking as well as drinking back at Fort Hell, when he'd been a contract scout. It had been his way of trying to fit in with others, though he'd been a fool to think he could ever fit in anywhere. Now, he just had some bad habits. His habit of imbibing in strong spirits had left a swath of broken up saloons and jail time in his wake.

He rolled the quirley tightly with his thick fingers, sealed it closed, returned the pouch to his shirt pocket, and thumbed a lucifer to life, holding the flame down behind a finger of rock jutting to his right. He inhaled deeply on the slightly stale Durham, which he'd been carrying since he'd left Cheyenne several months ago, and sat back against the stone wall.

He smelled her first.

The pleasant sweetness of nearly ripe chokecherries mixed with the primitive musk of woman. There was a footfall, and then her voice: "Yakima? It's me."

He remained sitting there, smoking, until he saw her shadow move in the starlit darkness to his left. She stood there for a time, looking down at him. At least, he thought she was looking at him. Her face was silhouetted against the starry sky above and behind her. The starlight flickered in her black hair.

"You couldn't sleep," she said.

"Restless, I reckon. That's all right. I thought I'd nod off a few times out here, after I had a smoke." He paused. When she didn't say anything, he said, "What about you? I thought you were asleep."

"With you waking up every ten minutes and reaching for your pistol? With that outlaw snoring like a bear in a cave?"

Yakima gave a wry chuff, blowing smoke into the darkness through his nostrils. "He really an outlaw?"

"Yes."

"Well, then I reckon I'd best keep an eye on him." Yakima narrowed an eye. "Or I reckon I could just shoot him. He's so sound asleep I doubt he even stirred when I left the camp."

"You could." She lifted her skirt and dropped to her knees beside him. "But why bother?"

She leaned toward him, and then she was in his arms, and her warm, moist lips were pressed against his.

13

She kissed him hungrily, poking her tongue into his mouth, entangling it with his. He felt her breasts against his chest, the nipples pebbling behind the thin cambric. Despite the thundering in his loins, he placed his hands on both sides of her head, and pushed her back, holding her there.

He stared at her, not saying anything, wondering through the fog of his desire what game she was laying out now. Her dark eyes were indecipherable. He knew one thing—he'd never want to play poker with her.

He chuckled, ran his fingers down through her long, coarse, straight hair, and rested his hands on slender shoulders. "All right," he said. "Go ahead."

"Go ahead with what?" she said, and he could see her brows ridge in the starlight. She placed a warm hand on his thigh.

PETER BRANDVOLD

"With what you're doing out here."

She lifted her hands toward his face, and he jerked with a start, grabbing both her wrists. He raised them to where he could get a look at them. In neither hand was a weapon.

He frowned, surprised.

She smiled a little sheepishly, shrugged and then turned and lay back against him, drawing his right arm around her, holding his hand in both of hers against her belly, gently caressing it with the backs of her fingers. "No tricks tonight, amigo. I came out here because I couldn't go back to sleep after you left."

"No tricks . . . Well, I'll be damned." He liked how she felt, leaning back against him, her warmth sliding into him, relieving his apprehension. "And the money?"

"Oddly, I care nothing about it anymore. Let MacElvy, whoever and whatever he is, have it."

Yakima craned his head to look at her, skeptical. "Why the change of heart?"

"I don't know. Why do you suppose? Maybe my heart has changed because it has been taken."

"Forgive my skepticism, Paloma."

She turned around, her face only inches from his, and sandwiched his head in her hands. "Tell me about the woman who has so marked this place for you, *mi amore*."

Very gently, she pressed her lips to his and then pulled

144

her face back slightly. "Tell me."

"Faith," he said. But it was almost like he hadn't said it. It was as though her name was always on the tip of his tongue, ready to slide out with the slightest nudge on his next breath. "She was my wife. A former workin' girl. Former whore. We weren't together long. But I loved her. Still do. Always will."

Paloma's dark eyes, inches from his, waited for him to continue. Her breath was a soft, easy rasp. Her breath caressed his chin. She was warm and pliant against him.

Yakima looked around her toward the night-cloaked desert. "Met her up in Colorado, took her away from her pimp, Bill Thornton. Thornton was right proprietary. He didn't like that. Didn't like a man, especially a breed, makin' off with his property. His men chased us. Makin' a long story short, we fought 'em off, came down here, Faith and I. Built up a ranch. Trapped wild horses in a canyon near here. Gentled 'em, sold 'em to the cavalry.

"The next year, Thornton's bounty hunters sniffed us out. They took Faith back up to Colorado, so Thornton could have the satisfaction of killin' her himself. I chased 'em but couldn't catch up to 'em until there was only about two breaths of life left in Faith. She died in my arms. But only after she'd killed Thornton"—he ground his teeth in remembered rage—"and burned him up in his saloon."

Yakima drew a deep, rattling breath, feeling moistness in his eyes. "I brought her back down here, buried her on our ranch." He looked at Paloma. "She's dust now. Just dust. Still, she's as real to me as you are, sittin' here tonight."

"You must have many fond memories of your time here, in the little shack, eh?" Paloma curled her lip insinuatingly.

Yakima smiled, remembering. "Yeah."

Paloma pressed her lips to his once more, kissed him for a time, grinding her breasts against his chest. Finally, she placed both her hands against his chest, and pushed away from him, rising. Her dress had come down, exposing one entire breast and most of the other. They were rising and falling heavily as she breathed.

"Don't worry, big Indio," she said, breathless, "I will not intrude on your memories."

She rose and pulled the straps of her dress up over her shoulders. She gave him a cockeyed smile and then turned away, the dress drawn taut across her round rump.

Yakima reached out, caught her wrist, and turned her around. He pulled her back down to him, hot blood surging through his lower regions, desire pulsing in his temples. He felt a hard knot of yearning in his throat—a yearning for this alluring woman before him, a yearning to be free of the long, imprisoning tentacles of remembered love gone forever.

"Like I said," he said, sliding the straps of Paloma's dress down her arms until both nubile orbs jiggled free of their confines, and he took them both in his hands, "she's dust."

***

Their fervid coupling was short but passionate.

She slumped against him, recuperating, breathing hard, for several minutes. She lifted her head and stared down at him, a celestial smile glittering in her eyes and pulling at her mouth. Her dress was bunched around her belly.

She waggled her hips against his, lowered her head to kiss him once more.

"I'm sorry, *mi amore*," she said in a throaty whisper.

He frowned. He was about to ask her what she meant, but then she raised her right hand above her head. He saw the rock too late. Before he could react, she'd smashed it against his right temple, laying him out cold.

***

Misery woke him.

He felt as though someone were smashing a sledgehammer against his head, over and over again. He opened his eyes, stretched his lips back from his teeth, and groaned.

He closed his eyes again, for the sun was blasting down at him. He could see the broad, lemon ball still blossoming against the backs of his eyelids, adding to his agony.

He rolled onto his side, raised a hand to his right temple. Oily with blood. Blood had dribbled down his temple and across his cheek to his jaw. It was partly dried to the texture of jelly.

When he'd taken several deep breaths to begin to start to quell the painful barking in his head, he sat up, pulled his pants up, and buckled his cartridge belt. He was surprised to find that his Colt was still in its holster. As bad as his head ached, she might have thought she'd killed him and seen no reason to take the revolver.

Or maybe she'd been too eager to get to the payroll loot to worry about something so insignificant as a gun.

Yakima groaned, cursed, and gained his knees. That caused a bayonet of razor-edged agony to slide between his ears, and he lowered his head to his hands, grinding his forehead into his palms.

"Crazy bitch!"

But then he realized that she'd only been doing what he should have expected her to try, and he redirected his anger toward himself.

"Damn fool!"

But it wasn't the first time his pecker had nearly gotten him killed. If he didn't die from the head-clubbing Paloma had given him, and which he felt was entirely likely, he'd vow to never trust another beautiful woman again.

He heaved himself to his feet, grinding his molars against the pain, and steadied himself against a boulder. The ground pitched and swayed. He squeezed his eyes closed, then slitted them, staring out across the desert. He thought he saw something move out there.

Shading his eyes with his hand, trying to ignore the sharp daggers the brassy sun stabbed at his eyes, he could see a dark shape far away on the butterscotch desert. The shape was little larger than a dust mote from this distance, but it was a horse and rider, all right.

It was her.

Had to be her.

Who else would be traveling alone out there?

She was riding southwest, likely heading for Mexico.

Yakima looked around, got his bearings, and then clamored down out of the rocks. When he turned at the bottom of the escarpment, Wolf was standing not twenty feet away from him, staring at him, the mount's molasses-colored eyes on either side of the white blaze on his snout vaguely incredulous, baldly condemning. The horse wore its halter, and the short length of rope the half-breed had used to tie him to the picket line dangled halfway to the ground. The stallion had been turned loose.

Yakima supposed he should have been grateful that

his gun and his horse were still with him, but he wasn't in the mood to feel grateful about anything. His neck was in far too big of a hump for that.

Little bitch wasn't going anywhere. Surely not the with the payroll loot. And surely not until he'd whipped her backside so she wouldn't be able to sit down without bawling for a month of Sundays!

Wolf shook his head and came running, nearly running Yakima over, who had to sidestep and dodge, cursing. Wolf ran past him, turned and stopped, shaking his head again and loosing a long whinny. Obviously, the horse was happier to see his rider than his rider was to see his horse.

"Thanks, you stupid cuss!" Yakima bit out, pressing the heel of his hand against his bloody temple. "What that little bitch started you wanna finish, huh? Christ . . ."

Wolf whickered, came over, and extended his snout toward his rider, sniffing at Yakima's bloody forehead.

"Yeah, she got me good."

Yakima started walking back across the little clearing in the direction of the shack, Wolf following close on his heels. The half-breed wondered what condition he'd find MacElvy in. As he approached the shack and the fire ring piled with gray ashes, however, he slowed his pace, frowning curiously. Not only was Paloma's gear missing from around the fire, but MacElvy's was, as well.

"I'll be goddamned," Yakima muttered.

He cursed again when he saw that his saddle scabbard, which was bent over a rock near his overturned saddle, was empty. He moved around the fire ring and cast a look down along the side of the shack still swathed in morning shadows though its thatched roof was limned with golden sunlight. Both the other two horses—MacElvy's and Paloma's—were gone.

Not surprising in light of the fact that the lawman's gear was gone.

Yakima looked at the shack. The strongbox was still there. He walked over to it, dropped to a knee, and opened the lid.

Empty.

Not surprising, either. They would have stuffed the loot into their saddlebags for easier packing.

Yakima swung back toward where Wolf stood twitching his ears near Yakima's gear, and felt the burn of indignation as well as a deep, sharp-edged chagrin. They'd thrown in together. He'd only seen one rider down on the desert, but there must have been two. He just hadn't seen the other one because of the sun glare.

He wondered when they'd paired up—before or after she'd gone out to the escarpment to bash Yakima's head in with the rock?

"Damnit," he said.

Wolf was staring at him, switching his tail slowly, curiously from side to side, as though to say, "What in hell have you gotten yourself into now?"

"Wolf," Yakima said, again pressing the heel of his hand to his forehead. "You're lookin' at a damn fool. I know you already know that, but you're right. You oughta pull foot and find you one with a nickel's worth of sense."

The horse momentarily stopped switching his tail and twitching his ears, staring at his rider. Then he resumed switching his tail again, still staring.

Yakima walked back to the stream, dropped to a knee, and bathed his temple, washing out what felt like a six-inch gash. He removed his neckerchief, wrapped it wound his head, and then set his hat down lightly on top of it. Wincing against the continuing throbbing, he gained his feet and walked back over to the camp.

MacElvy or Paloma had taken his Yellowboy repeater. That added to the rage already stoked inside the half-breed. He valued the Winchester almost as much as his horse. They were about the only two things of value he had.

At least they hadn't taken his horse or anything else, he saw, looking around at his gear. They'd wanted to travel lightly and leave as small a trail as possible. But even if they'd tried to take Wolf, the black wouldn't have gone, and there wasn't a mule alive more stubborn than the black.

Cursing and grunting, Yakima threw his saddle onto Wolf's back, and buckled the latigo. He stuffed his gear into his saddlebags, rolled his blankets up in his rain slicker and the four-point capote he wore in cold weather, and secured the bags and bedroll behind the saddle.

Right there was all he owned in the world. It was light by one Yellowboy repeater.

He swung heavily into the saddle and sat still for a moment, waiting for the hammering in his skull to abate. He remembered that soft, sensual look in her dark eyes—a half a second before she's smashed that rock against his head.

She'd left him for dead. MacElvy must've believed that she'd left the half-breed dead in the rocks. The lawman had probably been too distracted by other things—namely the money and the woman's supple body she'd no doubt promised him—to have investigated and finished the job she'd started.

"He'd live to regret that."

Yakima touched spurs to the stallion's flanks, and loped off across the clearing toward the forest and the way back down out of the mountains.

"They both would."

14

Something was running through the creosote, coming fast on Yakima's left.

The half-breed jerked back on Wolf's reins and slipped his Colt from its holster, raising the barrel and clicking the hammer back. The soft drumming sounds grew louder. It was accompanied by rasping pants and the occasional scrape of a creosote branch, the grinding of gravel.

Suddenly, the oak shrubs moved ahead and left, between two barrel-sized boulders, and something gray and brown darted through them and into the trail. The coyote stopped suddenly, flicked its head with raised ears and close-set, fear-sharp eyes toward the half-breed, gave a startled yip, and then, tucking its bushy trail firmly between its hindlegs, dashed into the brush on the trail's opposite side.

Yakima looked around. Escarpment loomed around

him, all turning dark now with the sun's westward plunge. He'd ridden hard all day, trying to ignore the hammering in his head until the hammering somewhat abated around noon, no thanks to the rough ride through the rocky, uneven terrain and the sun's relentless assault. It was a testament to his will that he'd folded up the pain and slid into a partially hidden drawer.

His eyes and mouth were dry as parchment, and he wanted a drink but was trying to conserve water because he didn't know where there were any springs out this way. He'd given Wolf a few drops here and there, and swabbed the black's nostrils with a moistened handkerchief. He figured he was close to the Mexican line, traveling cross-country, avoiding trails, because that's what the two riders he was tracking were doing.

Normally, he'd have filled two or three canteens for a trip out here. Unfortunately, he hadn't had the benefit of knowing he'd be making such a trip ahead of time.

He peered off in the direction from which the coyote had run. Something had frightened the beast.

What?

Yakima booted Wolf ahead and turned him right through an opening in the chaparral. He kept his cocked Colt aimed straight out over his horse's head, and he shuttled his gaze from left to right. Finally, seeing nothing, he stopped the horse.

He'd felt Wolf's back expanding and contracting nervously beneath the saddle since he'd seen the coyote. Maybe it was only the coyote that had spooked him. But now the horse gave his tail a hard swish and jerked his head up, whickering. He dug a front hoof at the ground. That set the hair bristling at the back of the half-breed's neck, his heartbeat quickening.

He looked around wildly, sweat sliding down the sides of his face from beneath his hat brim, carving runnels through the desert dirt coating him.

"Psssst!" came a voice somewhere to his right.

He jerked his gaze in that direction. All he could see were tufts of prickly pear and barrel cactus and clumps of cat claw and desert oak amidst the taller creosote shrubs, ocotillo, and saguaro.

"Ya-ki-ma!" came the hissing voice, causing Wolf to whicker again and lurch.

Yakima continued to look around wildly, his desperate gaze probing every mound of gravel and boulder and sandstone dyke thrusting itself up out of the red caliche. "Who . . . who . . . the hell . . . *where* the hell—?"

The hiss was louder this time: "*Look out!*"

Yakima turned to see an Apache diving at him from halfway up a sandstone scarp sheathed in Mormon tea and cat claw and behind which the warrior must have been hunkering. The brave gave a loud, coyote-like bark and then gritted his teeth as he swung the feathered war hatchet in his left fist. Yakima dropped his Colt and grabbed the Indian's right wrist as the brave slammed into him. He stopped the war hatchet's arc toward the opposite temple that Paloma had likely scarred for life, with about one cat's whisker of room to spare!

The Apache grunted and wheezed as he drove Yakima from his saddle, both going airborne, groaning and grunting, clinging to each other like two lovers after a long separation. The ground rose up fast to smack Yakima hard about the back of his head and his shoulders.

Despite the reignited fire in his right temple, he managed to keep his right hand wrapped around the Apache's left hand wielding the hatchet, and jab his left fist against the brave's jaw. That took some of the demonic delight out of the brave's dark eyes. The brave blinked and rolled half over. Yakima slammed his left fist into the brave's face two more times before the brave released the war hatchet.

The brave gave another loud yip, his long, coarse hair flying around his head. He had just started to wrap both his hands around Yakima's neck when his eyes opened wide in shock.

His eyes rolled down in their sockets to stare at the Arkansas toothpick that the half-breed had just slipped into his neck, just right of the warrior's Adam's apple. The

157

brave's mouth opened, and, rising to his knees, a horrified expression scrunching up his sandstone-colored face, he flailed both hands at the hide-wrapped handle of the knife sticking out of his throat.

"Here, let me you help you," Yakima said with a grunt, reaching up to pull the toothpick out of the brave's neck.

Blood geysered as the blade slipped free. More blood oozed out the brave's open mouth before Yakima gained his feet and kicked the brave over backward.

Instantly, more war whoops rose shrilly, sounding as though Yakima were being surrounded by rabid coyotes. Rifles belched. Bullets plumed the dust and gravel around the half-breed's moccasins, chewing into cholla plants and snapping oak branches.

Crouching, Yakima looked around for Wolf. No sign of the beast. Normally loyal to a fault, the black wasted no time in fleeing Apaches. He was long gone. But then Yakima remembered that the horse wasn't carrying his Yellowboy, anyway.

He saw his still-cocked Colt lying under a greasewood. As the rifles continued to belch and the braves continued to whoop and bullets plunked into the ground around his moccasins, Yakima dove on the piece, and rolled. He pushed up on his butt, extending the revolver before him, and fired through ocotillo branches.

A brave yowled and fell.

He fired again and a brave yipped and flew backwards off an escarpment.

Yakima found another target, and fired, not sure if he'd hit his mark or not. There were two many figures dancing amongst the brush and cacti, too many dark-skinned, loin-cloth clad braves running toward him from the chaparral, some flinging arrows, others shooting old-model Army carbines.

He got up and ran, dropped when several bullets screeched past his head, and rolled. He came up firing from a knee until his hammer clicked on an empty chamber. He tossed away the Colt, grabbed the old Spencer carbine of one of the braves he'd killed, and dodged behind a boulder.

He pressed his back to the boulder, pricking his ears, listening.

The firing had stopped. He gritted his teeth against the searing pain that was roaring like a wounded lion in his head, and tried to listen for the Apaches. As he did, he worked the carbine's trigger guard cocking mechanism—he'd used the same model back when he'd been a contract scout—and drew the heavy hammer back to full cock.

"Behind you!" a pinched voice called.

He turned to his right, edged a peek around the side of his covering boulder. A crouching brave stopped dead in his tracks, raised his Springfield trapdoor carbine, and fired. Yakima drew his head back behind the boulder as the .45-caliber bullet smashed loudly into the rock where his head had been. Yakima stepped out from behind the boulder and fired his seven-shot Spencer from his waist.

The Apache dropped his own carbine, doubled over and kicked up dust as Yakima's bullet drove him five feet back. Yakima fired the Spencer again, the .52-caliber ball smashing into the black crown of the Apache's skull, where the hair had been parted into separate braids.

The brave crumpled into a bloody, quivering heap.

Yakima quickly cocked the Spencer once more and sidestepped, pivoting from the hips and looking around. Dust wafted, acrid with the smell of fresh blood and burnt powder. He heard nothing but distant birds until hoof thuds rose.

He ran around an escarpment and saw three braves galloping up a slight rise to the north, each leading several riderless mustangs behind them. One glanced over his shoulder, showing his white teeth through a grimace, and then turned his head forward and lowered it, batting his moccasin-clad heels against the ribs of his short-legged coyote-dun.

The braves topped the rise and disappeared down the other side, their tan dust sifting behind them.

Holding the cocked Spencer's butt against his hip, Yakima walked slowly back in the direction from which he'd come. He scowled into the brush, looking for the bearer of the voice who'd warned him both times. But nothing moved in the chaparral.

"Breed!" rose the voice again.

Yakima stopped, looked around. He could see nothing but rocks and shrubs. It was as though someone were toying with him.

"Yakima, over here, damnit!" said the voice he could not recognize nor pinpoint.

"Where?"

"Here. To your right. I mean, *left!*"

Yakima moved slowly to his left. He passed a droopy mesquite, moccasins crunching on the fallen beans, and stopped.

"Here I am!" the voice said as though from only a few feet away. "Right here. Careful so you don't kick me!"

"Still don't see you."

"Look down."

Yakima looked down. All he could see was a rock about the size of a man's head resting on a mound of soft desert sand. But then the rock moved—at least the lower half of it moved. Yakima jerked with a start, and tightened his grip on the carbine.

But then he saw that the rock was not a rock at all. It

was a head. A human head. And what had moved were the man's badly chapped, pink lips. They'd formed a smile.

"MacElvy?"

The lips formed another smile. The man's eyelids fell and rose. One eye was bloody. The man's hair was mashed flat against his skull, showing the indentation of his hat. "Give a fellow traveler a hand?"

Yakima glanced around once more and then off-cocked the carbine and lowered it. Anger flamed in him once more. "Why in the hell should I?"

"Well, because I'm buried to the neck and I do believe there might be fire ants down here around my privates." MacElvy blinked his good eye, and winced. The other, bloody eye remained closed.

"Where's your partner?"

"My ... who ...?"

Again, Yakima looked around, scanning the chaparral now for the woman instead of Apaches. "Paloma. Where is she?"

"Hell, she was a good hour, maybe two hours ahead of me."

"Huh?"

"Yeah, she tried to shoot me while I was still in my blankets. Her bullet chewed off my earlobe but left me otherwise intact. But she ran my horse off. Ran both our horses off. Took me just north of forever to run mine down, after she high-tailed it with the loot. I thought you was dead! Didn't you hear the shootin' and then me *callin'*? I called for you several times before I lit out after her. Figured you was *dead*, like she tried to do to *me!*"

Yakima narrowed a skeptical eye. He was damn tired of being made a fool of though he knew he'd had plenty to do with that himself. "You sure you and her didn't throw in together? Didn't decide you'd head down to Mexico with the loot and live high on the hog?"

"Hell, no! That's her in your head again! Look, could you dig me out of here before the fire ants start chompin' into my balls. We can palaver all you want after that. Those damn Chiricahuas was just about to slice off my eyelids before they heard you comin'. Let the sun cook my eyeballs like poachin' oysters. Nasty devils! They'd just started slicin' on my right one, and my eye's so full of blood I can't see out of it. Christ! I'm am so goddamn unenthusiastic about this mission, I'm ready to pull my picket pin and ride back to Prescott and tell the Chief Marshal he can shove my badge so far up his ass that . . .."

He let his voice trail off as Yakima started to dig with the butt of his carbine.

"Oh, thank you. Thank you. There will surely be a place for you in Heaven. I will see to that myself."

"Don't do me any favors, MacElvy. I've been lied to so many times I still don't know what to think."

"Not by me you haven't!"

"Just shut up and let me dig."

"Hey, that forehead of yours looks nasty. Does it hurt?"

Yakima stopped and gave him a look of severely strained patience.

"Right," said MacElvy. "I'll shut up and let you dig."

15

Just after sundown, Paloma stopped her buckskin on a rise from which she'd been hearing the patter of piano music for nearly the last mile or so. Now she saw where the music was coming from.

Below, a pale ribbon of wagon road—probably a freight road—curved through the desert that was spruce green and burnt orange now in the last light. On the far side of the wagon road from Paloma stood a sprawling structure composed of wood and mud bricks. It must have been three stories tall. The sun had gone down behind it, a bright splash of yellow behind the mountains that stood black against it.

Against the mountains stood this large structure, all of its windows lit against the coming night. On the broad front gallery, two hanging lanterns swung back and forth in the rising night breeze, squawking on their rusty chains. In the large yard fronting the place were a dozen wagons of every shape and size, some with mules or horses standing hipshot in the traces.

There was a small barn behind the place with an adjoining corral in which more stock milled. A burro was braying raucously as it hung its head over the corral rails, staring toward the large building from which the cacophony rose. It either didn't like the noise or it was calling its owner.

At the same time, a horse—probably a stallion—was rising up onto its back legs and whinning loudly, aggressively, probably bedeviling another mount trying to get away from it. A mare, no doubt. The stallion looked black against the sunset, its glistening mane buffeting in the breeze. Pink dust rose around the stallion's hooves, disappearing like vapor against the heavy, growing shadows.

The stallion caused Paloma to think of the fine halfbreed stallion she'd coupled with to such great satisfaction the night before. She glanced over her should warily. For some reason, she'd sensed that he was trailing her though she'd been certain that she'd killed him with the rock. She'd smashed him hard enough to kill most men. Probably Yakima, as well.

But now, sensing him behind her, she had her doubts. She should have checked to make sure.

She turned her head back forward and shook her

breeze-jostled hair back behind her ears. No, he was dead, all right. A shame for such a man to be dead, but now the money was hers, and no one would stand in her way of finally attaining the rich life she'd always yearned for, striven for.

She'd spent two years with that fetid javelina otherwise known as Clancy Brewer. For two years, she'd let him mewl around between her legs, taking his satisfaction in haste and giving her absolutely none in return. In fact, he'd given her absolutely *nothing* in return. Which was why she'd been so happy when the handsome outlaw rake, Octavio La Paz, had come along.

She sensed that now her luck was changing, though she had to admit she wished it had changed *with* Yakima instead of *against* him. Some men just wouldn't listen to reason. If he'd given Paloma half a chance, she could have made that half-breed drifter's life so much better . . . in more ways than one.

No point in thinking about what might have been. She needed to keep looking ahead. And that's what she did now as she considered the noisy building sitting below. It was likely a roadhouse. Probably a brothel, as well. She could probably get a warm meal and something to cut the trail dust down there.

And likely a hot bath, as well. She had enough money for just about anything she wanted.

The only problem was that anywhere there were men—especially drinking men—there would likely be danger, as well. Oh, well. Not taking a chance now and then never got a girl anywhere. Besides, Paloma was no shrinking violet. She swung down from her buckskin's back, reached into a saddlebag pouch, and pulled out a holstered pistol and cartridge belt. The gun had been in the saddlebags she'd acquired back at the rustlers' camp. A fortunate happenstance for Paloma. A beautiful girl on the run with a hundred thousand dollars had best arm herself against snakes.

Especially human *male* snakes.

She wrapped the belt around her lean waist. She had to notch the very last hole, and even then the gun dropped low on her hip. She unwrapped her striped serape from around her blanket roll, and dropped it over her head. Fortunately, the man-sized poncho fell to nearly her knees, hiding the gun and holster. It was also baggy enough that the gun didn't bulge to an overly obvious degree.

Now, most importantly, what was she going to do about the loot?

She couldn't very well waltz into the roadhouse with the saddlebags draped over her shoulder. No, that wouldn't do. Just herself alone—a *beautiful young woman alone*—would attract enough attention without dressing herself in a hundred thousand dollars of stolen army payroll money.

Quickly, she looked around. When she found what she was looking for, she led her horse over to a niche in a small pile of rocks along the trail's left side, just back from the brow of the hill and out of sight from the roadhouse. She pulled the saddlebags off the buckskin's back, hauled them around a palo verde and over to the niche sheathed in cactus.

She removed a packet of greenbacks from one of the pouches, buckled the flap, and then shoved the saddlebags deep into the niche. It was so dark that she couldn't see them now by night; she hoped that they would not be seen by day, either. Anyway, they were far enough off the trail that anyone spying them would have to be looking for them.

That task accomplished, she stuffed the packet of bills down her dress and into her cleavage. A lascivious thrill bit her, spread a warmth through her belly, and she smiled sensuously as she strode back over to the buckskin, and swung up into the saddle. Having that much money snuggling in her cleavage was even better than having a handsome man nuzzle her breasts.

She put the buckskin down the gradual slope and rode on into the roadhouse yard. The piano music grew louder as did the low roar and laughter of the customers whose silhouettes she could see swaying and jostling through the red-curtained windows. Now she could see in the lamplight shed by the window a large sign over the place's broad front veranda announcing KING'S FORK SALOON. Smaller letters below the larger ones read, "Kingston Ballantrae III, Prop."

There were several hitchracks on each side of the sprawling building, all festooned with saddled horses standing hang-headed and droopy tailed, saddle cinches dangling so the patient beasts could breathe freely while their riders drank and frolicked. Vaguely, as she turned the buckskin toward the lesser populated of the hitchracks on the building's left side, Paloma wondered where all these people hailed from. The land stretching away from the roadhouse in all directions was a vast, dry desert broken by ravines and canyons and lumpy with various mountain ranges—home, she'd always thought, to not much more than coyotes, mountain lions, and Apaches.

Mexico, she believed, lay just south. How far away, she wasn't sure. She hoped to inquire inside about that as well as about the distance to the Sea of Cortez, where she intended to buy a ticket for a steamship ride up the west coast to San Francisco. With the army payroll loot, she'd buy a home there in that beautiful city on the bay, which she'd heard much about, seen pictures of, and had dreamt of one day living in.

She'd start her own business and take up with a handsome, wealthy man.

Adjusting the holster hanging low on her right hip beneath the serape, she climbed the porch steps. There were three or four men lounging in the shadows outside the saloon's batwing doors, smoking. They'd been talking when she'd ridden up. Now they'd fallen quiet as they studied her over the glowing coals of their cigarettes and cigars.

Paloma pointedly ignored them as two stepped reluctantly aside for her, and she pushed through the heavy, scrolled, oak louvre doors into the two front panels of which had been carved the shape of a king's crown. She stopped just inside the vast main drinking hall, and shoved her sombrero off her head, letting it hang by its hemp thong down her back.

She glanced quickly around the impressively appointed, rollicking place and then maneuvered her way through the crowd toward the large, ornate, horseshoe-shaped bar at the front of the room being tended by three bar tenders in white shirts, sleeve garters, stylish brocade vests, and ribbon bow ties. Another bar ran along the right wall, manned by two more barmen.

The crowd was mostly male, of course—a colorful mix of gringos as well as Mexicans. Paloma spied a few

Negroes, as well. Most appeared to be cattlemen or freighters. Five or six men in the blue uniforms of the U.S. cavalry were playing poker at a large, round table in a smoky corner. Two of the soldiers had scantily, brightly clad girls lounging on their laps.

Seeing the soldiers, Paloma grew conscious of the money snugged in the deep cleavage between her breasts, and she brushed a hand across the holstered revolver that hung heavily off her hip.

Men stepped aside for her, favoring her with their goatish gazes, eyes raking her up and down. She did not meet any of the gazes directly, for she'd learned when she'd first started acquiring the curves of a woman that doing so often attracted unwanted attention.

She wanted as little attention as possible here. Food, drink, a room, and a hot bath would do nicely, and she wanted to acquire them with no pomp or circumstance.

Two more men and a dove in a sheer pink dress through which Paloma could see everything, stepped aside for her, and she bellied up to the bar. It took a few moments for her to catch the eye of one of the busy bar tenders, but when she did the tall man with pomaded hair and a waxed mustache hustled right over.

"Evenin', Senorita. What can I get for you, this fine evenin'?" Leaning forward on his elbows, he winked lasciviously.

"A double shot of tequila. I assume you rent rooms?"

"We sure do rent rooms."

"I would like a double shot of tequila, a quiet room, a plate of food delivered to my room as well as hot water for a bath."

The barman frowned as he glanced around her and then he raked her once more with his oily gaze, and said, "You all alone?" They both had to raise their voices to be heard above the low roar of the crowd and the continuing patter of the piano from somewhere to Paloma's left. Somewhere to her right, a woman kept cackling raucously as though at the funniest jokes she'd ever heard.

"I can get you the drink and the room," the barman said. "As for the bath—we're a little busy right . . ."

He let his voice trail off as Paloma reached down the wide neck of the serape, and pulled the packet of bills out of her cleavage. She couldn't help flashing the money. She'd always wanted to be rich and now she was. While she knew it was dangerous for her to let anyone know how much money she was carrying, she acknowledged the admonition with only half of her brain. The other half, which enjoyed the surprised look on the barman's pockmarked face, overrode the less powerful, more prudent half.

Slowly, luxuriating in the man's admiring, incredulous stare, she peeled a ten-dollar note from the packet. As she did, she glanced to her right to see another man staring down at her from the balcony over the other bar. The man had thick, wavy blond hair that fell to his shoulders. He was maybe thirty-five or forty, well-built and handsome, with dark-blue eyes. He wore a flashy, burgundy suit with a double-breasted, gold-buttoned corduroy coat. A gold chain drooped from a watch pocket. The man was smoking a small cheroot tucked into the end of a long, wooden cigarette holder.

He stared down at Paloma with one eye narrowed, a faint smile tugging at one corner of his mouth. And then, drawing musingly on the cigarette holder, he turned away from the balcony rail and the several men he'd been standing with. Paloma returned her attention to the barman and set the ten-dollar note down on the bar.

"Will that cover it?" she asked, giving her nose a snooty tilt.

The barman leaned farther forward and laid his hand over the bill, covering it, and glanced sheepishly around. "For that much money, I'll run back to the kitchen and fetch the hot water myself. Say, uh, who are you anyway? Haven't seen you in this neck of the desert."

"Rest assured you never will again, amigo," Paloma said. "Now, if you don't mind—my drink and my room key. I will wait here while you prepare my bath. Vamos, por favor." She gave a regal smile. She'd been wanting to give a smile like that—a rich woman's smile—for most of her life. While she'd had money a time or two, she'd never had even half as much as she had now, and as she returned the packet to its niche between her breasts, she felt the burn of the bills in her brain.

Eyeing her shrewdly, the barman grabbed a tumbler off a pyramid, filled it to the brim with tequila, winked at her, and set the short, heavy glass down on the mahogany. He turned away for a moment, and then turned back and set a small, gold key engraved with the numb 23 down beside the tequila. He'd taken the ten-dollar note off the bar and slipped it into a pocket of his brocade vest. Now, he said, "Your room . . . and your bath . . . will be ready in twenty minutes. Shall I . . . hang around and wash your back?"

"I doubt that all these customers will allow you to spare that much time away from the bar, amigo," Paloma said, raising her shot glass to her mouth in a mocking salute.

His cheeks colored as he turned away, and, wiping his hands on his apron, hustled through swinging doors into what was probably the kitchen. As he did, several customers with empty glasses berated him and cast her angry glances. Trying not to smile her satisfaction, Paloma scooped the room key off the bar, closed her upper lip over the rim of the tumbler, and sipped the tequila.

It burned pleasantly in her throat and chest, behind the comforting weight of the bills. She was about to take another heady swallow when a man's soft, resonant voice said in her right ear, "Shame, shame, shame on you, Senorita."

16

Paloma jerked with a start.

She turned her head to see the handsome, burgundy-clad man from the balcony standing beside her. He was drawing on the cigarette holder from the corner of his mouth and arching a brow at her.

She drew a steady, calming breath and regarded him with faint disdain, as though he were intruding. "Shame on yourself. You're standing awfully close, you know?"

He chuckled, spewing smoke from his mouth as well as from his nostrils. Obviously, he hadn't been expecting such an impudent admonition, and he'd found it delightful, coming from such pretty lips. When he'd gathered himself he said, "You've distracted one of my very busy bar tenders. May I ask why?"

Coolly, Paloma raised her tequila glass and then showed him the key in her hand. "And food and a bath to go with the room."

"Ah, you're renting a room," said the man in the burgundy suit, taking another puff from his cigarillo. "Then all is forgiven." He smiled and extended his right hand to her. "Allow me to introduce myself. I am Kingston Ballantrae, proprietor of this old watering hole." His smile broadened with pride, his dark-blue eyes flashing in the lantern light.

She allowed him to squeeze her hand though she continued to regard him with faint disdain though he'd suddenly piqued her interest. Handsome, wealthy men didn't grow on trees. "Paloma Collado," she said off-handedly, rolling her eyes around. "Some watering hole you have here, amigo."

"Why, thank you, Senorita Collado. It is Senorita, I take it?' Still clinging to her hand, Balantrae glanced around as though her husband might be lurking behind him. "Or is there a Senor Collado?"

"There is no Senor Collado. What on earth would I want with a man?"

Ballantrae regarded her wistfully. "You aren't from around here, are you, Senorita?"

"Do I look like I would be from around here?"

He appeared to take that as an invitation to look her up and down though he did so with customary male lasciviousness. He chuckled. "No, no—I'll say you don't look like you'd hail from this neck of the desert. At least, I've never seen you before. And I assure you I am not a man who forgets a pretty face."

"How lovely for you."

"Where might you be from . . . if I'm not being rudely inquisitive . . .?"

"Most people tend not to stick their noses in other people's business," Paloma said again snootily, "but since it's been a long ride and I've spoken to no one for several days except my horse and the jackrabbits, what the hell? I am from a little village on the Yaqui River called Orozco."

"Mhmmm . . . never heard of it. But I'm afraid I don't travel often south of the border. My establishment here keeps me hopping, if you know what I mean."

"I'm sure it does."

He hesitated as though sheepish about continuing his inquiry. "And . . . what does such a beautiful young senorita do in this village of Orozco, and, furthermore, what is she doing so far away from home . . . *alone?* That's quite extraordinary, is it not—a beautiful young woman traveling alone through this bandito- and Apache-infested desert?"

She just realized that he had a faint English accent.

Paloma's mind was nimble. Without hesitation—automatically, in fact—the lie flowed like water over her lips. "My family was murdered recently by Apaches.

Finding myself alone, I took the money my father made while working in a silver mine north of the border, and left Orozco. I am on my way to live with my grandmother in Tucson."

In fact, she had been born in Orozco, and she did indeed have a grandmother in Tucson, but she hadn't seen the old bat in years and had no intention of ever seeing her again.

"She is alone, as I am, and she is old and decrepit," Paloma continued. "I will live with her and care for her until she dies. I have enough money to make us both quite comfortable."

"What a sweet girl you are."

"Don't be silly. Any girl would do such a thing for their grandmother, Senor Ballantrae."

"The trails are dangerous, my sweet."

"Don't I know it! I had to run my horse hard to escape two separate sets of banditos. And I saw the smoke of Apache signal fires in the distance, two days in a row." Paloma sipped her tequila, swallowed, licked her upper lip and savored the look he gave her, watching her tongue. She shook her head. "I am not worried, though. My horse is fast. Speaking of him, I can stable him in your barn?"

"Certainly!" Ballantrae looked around the room and then, apparently finding who he was looking for, chomped down on his cigarette holder and clapped his hands twice loudly. A short, stocky young man in a cheap suit limped over to them. He was carrying two trays of empty glasses and bottles. Probably a swamper. There were several such men shambling about the room, cleaning tables, emptying spittoons, and hustling drinks from the bar.

Ballantrae asked Paloma to identify her horse, and when she did, the saloon owner ordered the swamper, David, to stable the buckskin in the barn and to tend him thoroughly, providing plenty of straw, water, hay, and a bait of oats.

When David had set the trays down atop the bar and limped away, Paloma said with an impressed arch of her right eyebrow, "That's two men I've now taken from their regular duties."

"I have plenty of help. Former desert rats, mostly. They work for cheap just to have a roof over their heads. Besides, a girl alone in the desert deserves all the comforts she can find. And I assure you, Miss Paloma, you will find all the comforts you require right here, under my humble roof." He favored her with a gentlemanly dip of his chin.

"Oh, I don't think it is so humble, Senor." She stopped and turned her head slightly, casting him a saucily suspicious gaze. "And what will you be expecting in return for these comforts, Senor Ballantrae?"

The handsome saloon owner exhaled the last drag from his cigarillo, plucked the stub from the cigarette holder, and dropped it into the nearest brass spittoon. "Merely that you dine with me this evening, Paloma. I dare say I've never met a young woman as lovely, enchanting, and brave, and I would very much like to learn more about you."

Paloma sipped the tequila again, maneuvered her tongue again, enjoying the way his eyes sort of crossed and lit up as he watched her. She swallowed, shrugged. "If the grub's on you, how can I refuse?"

"Not only the grub, my dear."

"Oh?"

"It's a surprise. Why don't you go on up to your room and have that bath Chester is heating for you, and I'll send your surprise up shortly."

***

Paloma didn't know what to make of Ballantrae's "surprise," whatever it was. But she enjoyed surprises as much as the next girl. As long as they weren't a bucketful of rattlesnakes, that was. She had to admit that she was enjoying the handsome man's ministrations, not to mention the free room and board for her horse.

Sure, she had plenty of money. But why spend it when she didn't have to? The trail had been lonely; it would get lonelier. She'd enjoy a night in the saloon owner's company.

And she'd bet that the supper she'd be eating with him would be tastier than any plate that ole Chester would send up from the kitchen. The tequila would probably taste better than the glass she'd just drank, too. If the man played his cards right, she might just sleep with him.

Why not?

Ever since her time with Yakima Henry, she'd felt a needling desire in the pit of her belly though she doubted any man could live up to the high expectations the half-breed had left her with.

She did not need to unlock the door to room 20. As she strode down the red-carpeted hall of the building's second story, the first-story crowd's racket muffled now behind and below her, she saw that her door was standing half-open. She nudged the door wide and stepped into the room.

Chester was just turning away from a long, deep, ornately painted copper tub up from which tentacles of steam unfurled against the ceiling that was mostly in shadow. More steam lifted from the now-empty wooden buck he was just now lowering to his side.

"You make friends right quick," Chester said, tugging on one of his bushy side whiskers. "The boss—he fancies you."

"Don't feel too badly, Chester," Paloma said, giving a teasing smile as she tossed her hat on a brocade-upholstered chair to her left. "You never had a chance, anyway."

Chester gave a dry snort and brushed past her toward the door. "I'll be back with another couple of buckets." He glanced over his shoulder, giving a leering smile. "And I'll help you out of those duds. Don't worry—it comes with the room!" He laughed and left.

"Thank you, Chester!" Paloma yelled as his footsteps retreated down the hall.

She crouched to dip a hand into the half-filled tub. Good and hot. She was eager to climb in, but she'd wait until Chester had finished filling it. She didn't want to get him overwrought by the sight of her beautiful body.

Strolling around the room, admiring the humble but comfortable furnishings, she found herself humming. She was in a good mood, and why shouldn't she be?

She was a beautiful, wealthy young woman about to take a luxurious bath in a pretty tub in this unexpected saloon and hotel out here in this vast desert. She had a rich, handsome man to wine and dine her this evening, and a large, comfortable bed to sleep in—if she didn't find herself sleeping in his, that was.

She gave a devilish chuckle at that as she ran her fingertips around the globe of a lit Tiffany lamp on a table by the small balcony door. What's more, she was bound to become even wealthier than she was now, because just as it took corn to grow more corn, it took money to grow even more money.

And what better place than San Francisco to plant her seeds?

The steam was making it overly warm and humid. Deciding to let some air into the room, she drew the heavy drape back from the glass balcony door. As she did, a shrill scream exploded from her throat and, gazing in horror at the, tall, pale, sombrero-clad figure staring in at her through the door's black glass, she stumbled backward, caught her boots on the rug, and fell to her ass.

"Holy shit!" Chester cried behind her, his shoes tapping on the rug. "You all right?"

He set his buckets down and crouched beside her. Paloma turned to him and grabbed his arm as though to a life raft, and then she turned back to the balcony door again. As she did, she jerked up the skirt of her serape and shucked her revolver from its holster.

"Oh, god—it's him!" she cried, lifting the heavy gun in her hand and fumbling with the hammer. "It's him! *Mierda!*"

"It's *who?*"

"La Paz!" She stared at the black glass glinting with the reflected light of the Tiffany lamp, and her brows ridged with a scowl. The face of Octavio La Paz was no longer there. There was only the darkness of the night pushing toward her, and the glass reflecting the umber lamplight.

But she'd been sure he was there!

His eyes had been bulging—one had been eggshell white—and his unusually pale face had been pocked with oozing sores . . .

Or . . . maybe she'd just imagined him . . .?

"I could have sworn I saw him there," she muttered in Spanish.

"Say again," Chester said. "No *sabe*."

Slowly, she lowered the pistol. "La Paz," she whispered to herself.

Chester glowered at her suspiciously. "*Octavio* La Paz? The old border bandit? That Mexican *killer?*"

Getting ahold of herself, Paloma turned to Chester. She swung the pistol toward him, as well, and clicked back the hammer. "Shut up. Not one word about this or I'll gut-shoot you!"

Chester raised his hands, palms out, and slowly straightened.

"Pour the water into my tub and get out!" Paloma ordered, rising.

Quickly, the barman picked up one of the buckets and poured it into the tub, staring at the gun she kept aimed at him. "Careful now," he urged. "That's a mighty big gun for such a delicate little hand."

"You be careful, you bastard. Remember—one word of this and I will gut-shoot you and leave you to die slowly, bellowing for your mother!"

When he'd emptied the second bucket into the tub, Chester backed away to the door. Turning, he grumbled, "Boss has got his hands full tonight," and he went out and pulled the door closed behind him.

Paloma went over to the door and locked it. Keeping the cocked pistol in her hand, she walked back over to the balcony door. Holding her free hand up to shield the glare from the lamp, she stared out. Finally, she opened the door, which squawked on its hinges, and stepped slowly out onto the narrow balcony.

She could hear the roar of the crowd and the raucous hammering of the piano coming up from below. Several burly men dressed in the jackboots, buckskins, and the broad-brimmed leather or canvas hats of freighters were milling in the yard amongst the big freight wagons, smoking, drinking, and laughing. They were mostly in silhouette though the light from the first-floor windows limned an occasional swatch of bearded cheek or a man's buckskin-clad shoulder or glinted in a laughing eye.

There were the intermittent red glows of cigarettes or cigars or pipe bowls. Tobacco smoke wafted on the nearly still, fresh night air that also owned the tang of the desert.

Paloma wanted to call down there to ask if anyone had seen a man climbing around up here, but nixed the idea.

She didn't want to attract any more attention to herself than she already had. Besides, they would likely think her crazy. And maybe she *was* crazy. Maybe the long ride in the hot desert sun had boiled her brains, and she had only imagined that Octavio had come back from the dead to take his revenge.

She'd been dreaming.

Of course, she'd been imagining Octavio. She'd left him dying from snakeroot poison. And she'd given him a liberal jigger of the stuff, too. No man could survive that!

Depressing the pistol's hammer, she dropped it into its holster. She gave a caustic chuff, mocking herself, and turned back toward her room. Something caught her eye, and she stopped, turned back toward the balcony, and dropped to a knee. She lowered her hand and touched a finger to the small, dark stain on the balcony's wooden floor.

She raised the finger to her nose, and sniffed the odor of fresh horse dung.

The fine hairs at the back of her neck bristled.

Chicken flesh rippled across breasts.

Slowly, she rose and turned to the yard. "Octavio?" she whispered.

She stood staring into the night for another full minute.

"No, silly girl," she said. "Octavio is dead. Someone else soiled the balcony. You've had too much sun, is all."

Trying to ignore the consternation causing her heart to quicken, she went back inside, closed the balcony door, and drew the heavy drapes closed.

17

"Did you like my surprise?" Ballantrae asked when Paloma had answered his knock on her door. "I know I do."
His eyes nearly crossed again, glinting, as he stared down
at the low-necked, silk and taffeta frock edged in gold that
clung to her body like a second skin. "I see it definitely
likes you, too, my dear."

"It is a beautiful dress," Paloma said, holding the wine-
red, gold-edged shawl about her naked shoulders. "Por
favor. It makes me feel much more like a woman than I
did in my dusty trail clothes."

The dress had been brought to her room by one of
Ballantrae's lovely ladies of the evening. The whore,
whose name was Candace, had helped Paloma into the
tight affair, and buttoned the back for her. She'd also
brought a bottle of fine Mexican tequila, and the two
young women had enjoyed a glass while Candace had

fixed Paloma's hair, adorning it with a ribbon the same wine-red as the frock and the shawl.

"Radiant," the saloon owner cooed, gravely shaking his head and furrowing his brows. "Absolutely radiant. I am still trying to imagine how such beauty could just walk in out of the desert."

He turned and crooked his arm for her. "Shall we stroll down to the dining room? I've given our order to the cook. I hope you like steak with all the trimmings. I thought we'd start with a bottle of French wine."

"Lovely."

Paloma took his arm and let him lead her along the hall. They dropped slowly down the stairs, and the piano's raucous hammering faded as the player caught sight of the handsome couple. All eyes followed his to the stairs, and the roared died gradually. The crowd stared in rapt attention, men elbowing other men and jerking their chins toward the stairs.

Paloma felt her cheeks warm under the scrutiny. It was not a bad feeling. She no longer cared if she was noticed. She welcomed it, in fact. She could imagine herself thrilling to a life filled with such fawning.

Only, she wanted the fawning to occur in a place like San Francisco, not a saloon brothel in the middle of the Sonoran Desert. The smelly desert rats and scantily clad, over painted percentage girls would probably gawk at a girl even half as beautiful wearing the wine-red frock.

Still, Paloma felt quite elegant, and her belly trembled at the thought of the bountiful life awaiting her. All made possible by those saddlebags she'd tucked away in the niche atop the northeastern ridge.

"Now, if that ain't a purty couple!" yelled a tall man standing at the bar. Obviously drunk, he turned full around to point at Ballantrae and Paloma with a half-empty whiskey bottle. "Yessir, that there is one damn purty couple. In fact, you two make damn near as handsome a pair as Miss Paloma and Octavio La Paz once did!"

Paloma jerked to a stop at the bottom of the stairs, releasing Ballantrae's arm. Gazing in shock and horror at the tall, horse-faced, bearded American at the bar, she slapped a hand to her cleavage, her heart hiccupping beneath her heaving breasts. The man who'd spoken—a tall gringo dressed in a flashy Mexican-style calico shirt and deerskin vest and deerskin leggings, and wearing a low-crowned, black and red sombrero—was none other than Octavio's former American partner, Kris Jorgenson.

Jorgenson was one of the several men whom La Paz had double-crossed when he'd killed several others in his gang and absconded with the stolen payroll money, keeping it all for himself.

"Hah! Hah! Hah!" the American border bandit roared, stomping one high-heeled, spurred boot down on the strip of bare floor running along the bar. He tapped the shoulder of a much shorter Mexican standing beside him, facing him, his back to Paloma. "Look there, Miguel! Don't ole Paloma look like she's seen a ghost?"

The short Mexican in a brown leather charro jacket turned his black-haired head toward Paloma, and spread his lips back from his large white teeth in a heavy-lidded, drunken smile.

"Miguel Cordoba," a voice whispered in Paloma's head.

And then she saw the rest of them—three others, one more yanqui and two more Mexicans lined up to either side of Jorgenson and Miguel Cordoba. The rest of the gang whom La Paz had double-crossed when they'd split up to evade the soldiers.

They were all in dusty, smoke-stained trail garb. They were dirty and sweaty and sunburned. They wore beards or mustaches and bright neckerchiefs, and they all had at least two pistols and a knife or two hanging from their shell belts. She'd seen them all several times before back in Horsetooth with Octavio though she remembered only the names of Jorgenson and Cordoba.

"What on earth is he talking about?" Ballantrae asked beneath Jorgenson's continuing guffaws, regarding Paloma dubiously. "Octavio La Paz? The *Mexican killer?*"

All the onlookers had been silent. Now, a quiet, collective noise of muttered exclamations rose, sounding like a wind playing in a near canyon. Paloma barely heard. She'd just become aware that Jorgenson had a pair of saddlebags thrown over his left shoulder. The saddlebags appeared terrifyingly familiar. The butterscotch-colored bag hanging down the tall man's chest had a torn flap, just as hers did. It was also bulging.

But those couldn't be *her* bags. She'd placed them in the niche out of sight from the trail. And no one had been around. No one could have possibly seen her . . .

But the glow in Jorgenson's pale blue eyes set deep beneath shaggy, pewter brows told her that *he* had seen. He and his men must have been shadowing her.

"No!" Paloma heard herself scream. "*No!*" She stumbled forward, broke into a run. "No, you bastard! Those are *mine!*"

Jorgenson laughed and dropped his hand to the long-barreled .45-hanging low on his right thigh. One of the swampers had been standing near the bar, a filled tray ready to be delivered to a table resting heavily in a hand raised above his head. He stepped forward into Paloma's path, as though to forestall the imminent skirmish, but got a bullet in the small of his back for his efforts.

The crash of Jorgenson's .45 caused every person in the room to jump.

Facing Paloma, the beefy, lazy-eyed swamper made a horrified expression. Stumbling forward, he dropped the tray, which went crashing to the floor.

Paloma screamed and threw her arms out as though to hug the swamper, and he fell into her, knocking her off her feet and falling on top of her as her back and the back of her head hit the floor with a loud thud despite the carpet.

Staring over the shoulder of the quivering swamper, Paloma screamed again as Jorgenson stepped toward her, cursing and clicking his .45's hammer back once more. At the same time, Chester pulled a sawed-off, double-barreled shotgun from beneath the bar, and shouted, "Hold it right there, you son of a—!"

The last word either died stillborn on his lips or was drowned by the thunder of Jorgenson's revolver, which the tall, gringo outlaw had swung toward Chester and fired.

Chester had not quite gotten his shotgun leveled before Jorgenson's bullet plowed through the dead center of his pretty brocade vest, just down from his bow tie. Chester screamed and, pivoting to his left, tripped one of the shotgun's two triggers, spewing buckshot into the crowd but not before shredding Miguel Cordoba's left ear and cheek and turning that eye the color of a ripe tomato.

Shrieking, Cordoba grabbed that side of his face while several innocent bystanders also bellowed furious complaints as the rest of Chester's buckshot found more flesh to tear.

Insane with pain and rage, Cordoba stumbled forward, screaming, clutching his bloody face, and grabbing a silver-chased revolver from its holster. Continuing to stumble forward, he began cutting loose with the Spanish epithets as well as the gun, firing willy-nilly into the crowd. Behind him, Jorgenson laughed and followed suit with his own Colt while the other three banditos unleashed their own hoglegs and followed the lead of the first two men.

Beneath the ear-rattling cacophony of thundering six-shooters and screaming men and women, Paloma could hear whom she believed to be Ballantrae shouting, "No! No! Stop shooting you fools!"

To no avail.

The shooting and screaming continued, the floor fairly leaping like a living thing being kicked beneath Paloma.

She grunted as she shoved the dying swamper off of her and rolled onto her belly, keeping her head low and holding her hands over her ears or surely the loud, booming reports would have shredded her eardrums. Bullets screeched and warmed the air around her as they plunked and slammed into tables and chairs and glasses and bottles, sending wood, glass, ashtrays, and playing cards spraying in all directions.

Paloma saw the piano and crawled for it, keeping one hand pressed to one ear. The piano player was slumped forward against the keys, his derby hat tipped forward against the open music book before him. Blood dribbled down the arm hanging straight down toward the floor at his side and forming a soggy pool on the rug near a leg of the bench.

Paloma made a face at the blood then crawled beneath the bench and hunkered there on her knees, clamping both hands over her ears, pressing her forehead hard against the rug.

Judging by the loudness of the varied din, every man in the room—every man still living, that was—was opening up with his own revolver. Amidst the cacophony, Paloma could hear a throaty-voiced woman bellowing, "Oh, you dirty bastards! Oh, you lousy, filthy-dirty bastards!"

Time slowed to a cold molasses drip. The gunfire seemed to continue as though it would never die. The musky odor of coal oil reached Paloma's nose, and she heard herself mutter against the floor, "Oh-oh."

Her dread was proven well founded. A moment later she smelled smoke. A lit lamp or lamps had been shattered, and a fire had started somewhere not far away from her.

She could feel the ominous heat of the flames. A man's shouts turned to agonized screams. Glancing up, Paloma saw a murky figure through the webbing powder- and fire smoke jostle violently. Flames were crawling quickly up both of the men's legs as he tried in vain to stomp them out.

Screaming even louder amidst the flashing and the roars of pistols, he started running but seemed to trip over something. He fell hard, his screams dying as the flames grew brighter, consuming him and spreading along the floor around his slumped figure.

They were growing even brighter, which meant they were probably heading in Paloma's direction.

The gunfire was dwindling as those men still living were running outside as were, judging by the female screams, the working girls. Paloma crawled out from under the bench and tried to stand, but the heavy fumes of the coal oil and the thickening smoke gushed down her throat like thick tufts of warm wool soaked in kerosene, cutting off her wind. She coughed, choked, nearly past out. Forcing herself to remain conscious, she started making her way toward where she thought the front door was located.

Many dead men impeded her way. She crawled over and around them, around tables and overturned chairs. She could hear the working girls sobbing and crying, could feel cool, fresh air threading through the thickening smoke. Coughing, trying to draw air down her badly constricted throat, she followed the sounds and the fresh air to the front door.

Rising to a crouch, she stumbled across the porch, down the steps, and into the yard that was nearly as smoky as the inside of the burning place. She ran, stumbling on the hem of her delicate dress, toward fresher and fresher air. Around her were other women either down on hands and knees or stumped forward, hands on their thighs, sobbing and coughing. In the distance, she heard men's yells and victorious shouts and the drumming of horse hooves.

Glancing to her right, she could see several horseback riders galloping out of the smoky yard lit by the fire's dancing flames, and into the darkness to the south of the roadhouse.

As they rode, they triggered pistols into the air.

She couldn't be sure because of the smoke and jostling shadows, but she thought Jorgenson, identifiable by his large black and red sombrero, was at the head of the pack, the saddlebags draped over his left shoulder.

"*Bastardo,*" Paloma choked out, grabbing at the coping around a large stock tank.

And then fatigue washed over her, and she collapsed.

18

Paloma woke to squawking sounds. The squawking was growing gradually louder.

She opened her eyes and immediately grimaced at the sun beating down on her. She raised a hand to shield it from her face, and when she got her vision to focus, she saw a wagon heading toward her.

It was a large, long, leather-seated wagon with a make-shift canopy made of what appeared gold-tasseled red drapes stretched over support posts. Two horses were pulling the strange contraption around from behind what remained of the burned down saloon—a pile of gray ashes and half-burned ceiling beams, a few scorched chimneys standing here and there amidst the rubble.

Smoke still rose from the massive ruin, some columns thicker than others. The yard around Paloma was littered with ashes. Her dress was charred and showed where cinders had landed on her. She was lucky she, too, hadn't caught fire while she lay out here in the yard, unconscious.

The wagon made a wide arc around the front of the saloon, avoiding boards and shingles and beams from the burned building that had fallen into the yard. The wagon, Paloma now saw as it drew near, was being driven by a dour-looking Kingston Ballantrae. He was wearing the same burgundy suit he'd been wearing last night, only today it didn't look half as sharp.

The man himself didn't look a third as striking. He was so dark with soot that he looked like a miner fresh from toiling in the earth's bowels. He wasn't wearing a hat, and his blond hair was sticking up in spikes around his head. Its ends appeared charred, as were his eyebrows.

Behind him, sitting sullenly in the wagon's four leather seats beneath the canopy, were at least a dozen soiled doves—all half-dressed in mostly underwear of all colors of the rainbow. They'd probably fled the burning building with what little they could hold in their arms, which hadn't been much. One girl wore merely a thin yellow wrapper and white pantaloons and black socks.

Ballantrae drew the wagon to a stop beside Paloma. He and the doves, including Candace, stared dully down at her. One was smoking a loosely rolled cigarette, curling her lips disdainfully at Paloma as she blew the smoke out from between her lips that were a mess of smeared pink lipstick.

Paloma had pushed up onto her elbows, staring sheepishly back at the group. Ballantrae continued to stare at her dully until finally he lifted his gaze above and beyond her, toward his once-grand, now-ruined hotel, and his lips formed a bitter expression. He shook the reins over the horses' backs, and the wagon lurched forward, ungreased wheel hubs squawking loudly. The girls turned their heads to stare back at Paloma as the wagon rolled on out of the yard, turned left onto the freight trail, and jounced off to the north, toward Tucson.

Paloma watched until the chaparral had absorbed it. Then she looked around once more. She was alone out here. There was only the massive ruin and the breeze ruffling the smoke and lifting dust and ash and throwing it at her.

She was alone. Her horse was gone. There were no horses anywhere around. All the corrals flanking the saloon had been emptied out, the gates thrown wide. A couple of tumbleweeds rolled in out of the desert, bouncing, and more dust lifted, and the wind caused the ruins to glow red in places, lifting cinders.

Paloma was alone and even poorer now than when Clancy Brewer was alive. Poorer than she'd ever been. Poorer by far than when she'd acquired the army payroll loot.

A sob exploded from deep within her chest. She rolled

onto her belly, buried her head in arms, and let the dam break. She bawled and bawled, tears dripping down her cheeks to form mud beneath her.

Muddy ash.

She bawled and bawled and bawled, occasionally kicking her black leather, side-button shoes that Ballantrae and Candace had outfitted her in, into the dust and ashes.

After a time, she realized that beneath her own wretched cries, she'd heard hoof clomps and felt the ground tremble slightly. Now a shadow slid over her. Apaches!

She whipped over onto her back.

No. Not Apaches. Yakima Henry was hunkered down beside her, staring dubiously down at her.

He was holding the reins of his black stallion, who stood behind him, also staring skeptically down at Paloma. Standing behind Yakima was MacElvy, a white, blood-spotted bandage over his left ear, a calico bandana angled across his forehead to cover his right eye. He had his thumbs hooked behind his cartridge belt as he stared beyond Paloma at the burned-down saloon. His white-faced brown horse flanked him.

The lawman looked down at Paloma over Yakima's left shoulder. "Girl," MacElvy said, chuckling dryly, "you leave a bloody trail and carve one hell of a wide swath!"

Another sob boiled up from Paloma's chest, and she twisted around and buried her head in her arms once more.

***

Later, when they'd set up camp in an arroyo south of the burned out saloon, where several sycamores and scrub oaks offered shade, Yakima stared down at the sullen-eyed, scantily-clad Paloma Collado and asked, "What're you gonna do with her?"

"What do you mean—what am I gonna do with her?" MacElvy tossing his saddle down near their small coffee fire with a grunt. "She shot my damn ear off. And because of her I damn near lost both eyelids!"

He glowered down at Paloma through his one good eye. She sat back against a scrub oak, her handcuffed wrists resting on her breasts that were all but exposed by the wine-red, gold-edged dress. She'd torn the skirt of the delicate dress, exposing nearly all of one fine-turned, olive-colored leg.

"That's a federal damn offense," the lawman said, "and she's goin' back to Prescott with me to answer for it. In irons!"

Yakima winced as he fingered the still painful cut on his forehead, which was still occasionally probing the area between his ears with a dull knife of agony. "Well, can't say as she don't deserve that or worse." He tossed the dregs of his coffee onto the fire, and heaved himself to his feet. "Me, though . . . well, I reckon I'll be ridin' on."

"Wait—where you goin'?" MacElvy asked, lifting the coffee pot away from the cup he'd been filling.

Yakima walked over to where Wolf stood ground-tied, latigo hanging beneath his belly, a feed sack draped over his ears. His Yellowboy was back in its sheath. Yakima had found it on one of the Chiricahuas he'd killed back near where they'd buried the lawman.

As he scrubbed out his cup out with a gloved hand, the half-breed looked off, pensive. "Not sure yet. Maybe I'll try San Diego for the winter. By spring, the law up north'll likely have forgotten about my little doin's. They got bigger fish to fry now with the West openin' up the way it is, railroads layin' track all over, and gangs like the James boys runnin' off their leashes."

He dropped the cup into his left saddlebag pouch.

"Hold on, now, breed . . . I mean, Yakima." MacElvy scowled over at him, his half-filled coffee cup smoking in his hand. "You can't just pull out on me. We have an agreement, damnit!"

"Hell, the money's gone. You heard her—Kris Jorgenson and the rest of his and La Paz's gang has it. Hell, they're probably well into Mexico by now, and they probably already got half the loot spent on mescal and senoritas."

"They can't be that far along. They rode out from the roadhouse last night. They're only a few hours ahead of us. You got to figure they probably didn't ride all night,

205

neither. Not out here in this scrub country with no moon to light their way."

Yakima was stripping the feed sack from over Wolf's ears, the stallion still trying to nibble every oat from the bottom of the bag. "The Old Mexican Road is a good trail. An old freight trail, leads all the way down to Mexico City."

"Hell, that bunch doesn't stick to the trails. With their reputations and haulin' that much dinero, they'll want to avoid the rurales and bounty hunters. Nah, they won't stick to the stage road. I'm guessin' they left the road by now and are headin' cross-country through the desert where they can't be tracked. There's a little village down by the Yaqui River they're likely headin' for. Isolated little place in rough country. It's where they hole up between jobs. They all got senoritas down there."

He gave Paloma a snide glance. "Includin' La Paz. Leastways, he did have . . . until someone gave him a drink that cored him like a damn apple!" He chuckled. "Had him one north of the border . . . and south of the border."

"Your mother laid with stinking mountain lions. She moaned for them. That's how you came to be, MacElvy." Paloma looked at Yakima. "Shoot him and take me with you. I will make it worth your while." She drew up her long, right leg, which exposed by the tear in her skirt. She glanced down at it and gave him a seductive wink.

Yakima gave a caustic snort as he stuffed the feed sack into the saddlebag pouch. "You've given me enough misery, senorita. Time to fork paths with you for good."

MacElvy straightened, tossed his half-filled cup away in frustration, and walked over to where the half-breed was reaching under Wolf's belly for the latigo. "Yakima, you can't abandon me out here. I got a job to do. I gotta get that money back from them outlaws, and there's too many for me to take on alone."

As he cinched the latigo. "You'd best ride to Fort Bryce and tell them soldiers your sob story. I'm through. Finished." He glanced at Paloma sitting there in her dirty, sooty, torn dress, her hair hanging wild about her face. It too was sooty and dusty. She looked as though she'd rolled in the stuff. "I'm done with both of you."

"That your final word?"

"That's my final word."

"Even though I could make sure you're granted amnesty for that killin' up north? I could do it, you know. I got pull with the local sheriffs up that way. Sheriffs *and* judges."

"Yeah," Yakima said, taking his reins and toeing a stirrup. "Even though." He heaved himself into the leather.

"My advice to you, MacElvy, is to—"

"I don't need your goddamn advice, breed!" the lawman spat out through gritted teeth. "I don't need nothin' from you. Not a damn thing. You been nothin' but a thorn in my side ever since I first laid eyes on you in the Horsetooth Saloon!"

He swung around, stumbled over a rock, cursed, and then picked up his coffee cup. Yakima watched him pick up the cup and use a leather swatch to remove the pot from the tripod over the fire, and fill the cup. Paloma stared back at Yakima through strands of hair hanging in her face. Her eyes were dark, glum. She was too crest-fallen to even bother pleading with him anymore.

As Yakima swung Wolf away from the camp, Paloma slowly turned her gaze back to the fire and stared down at it, the very picture of dejection. Yakima touched spurs to the stallion's flanks and rode on down the arroyo. He glanced back over his shoulder toward the fire. MacElvy sat there on the opposite side of the small flames from Paloma, tenderly touching the bandage over the ear she'd shredded.

A sorrier-looking pair he'd rarely seen. With one eye covered, one ear shredded, his face swollen from the buckshot pellets, MacElvy was in no condition to fight a small gang of border banditos. He had about as much chance of getting the stolen payroll money back by himself, with the handcuffed woman in tow, than he had of flying to the moon.

But he was too damn stubborn to give up.

Which meant he was going to get his fat ass killed, and Paloma right along with him. Why that mattered on iota to him, after all she'd done to him, he had no idea. Some-foolish-how, it did.

"Goddamnit!"

Yakima swung Wolf around, cursed again, and booted the horse back into the camp and stopped him. MacElvy and Paloma turned to him, hopefully.

Yakima snarled, "If you're that bound and determined to get yourself killed, we'd best at least get her a horse, because she sure as hell ain't ridin' double with me!"

19

Three days later, Yakima held Wolf's reins as he dropped to a knee on the steep, rocky slope they were on. He plucked a horse apple out from a small slice of shade beside a rock, and sniffed. He pinched the apple. It did not come apart but merely compressed like semi-wet clay.

He looked up the slope toward several large sandstone knobs capping the mountain, beneath a Mexican sky the color of blue porcelain and just as flawless. The copper-colored knobs were marked by many caves semi-hidden by boulders that had tumbled down over the centuries from the top of the caprock.

The area had been home to some ancient people. Yakima had seen the petroglyphs they'd left behind, and broken clay pottery marking where they'd camped at one time, or where they'd built their homes. He'd also found discarded horns they'd apparently used as utensils of one kind or another, preserved by the dry air.

He shuttled his gaze across the caves, most sitting low against the knob, and felt a cool spider of menace scuttle up his spine, beneath his sweat-soaked calico shirt. "They've been through here, all right," he said. "Not long ago. Maybe two, three hours ago."

MacElvy was leading his horse toward Yakima from about thirty yards downslope. Paloma was ahead of him and to his left a bit, also walking her horse, a steeldust gelding with three black socks which they'd rundown in the desert. It was saddled and bridled, so it had likely belonged to one of the men who'd burned up in the saloon fire.

MacElvy doffed his hat and scrubbed his pale forehead with a grimy shirtsleeve. "I told you they'd cut through these mountains. Short cut to the Yaqui River and that village they hole up in."

Yakima grimaced and said, "Keep your voice down."

MacElvy stopped suddenly and stared up the slope toward the caprock. "You think they're up there? Kinda early to camp."

"If we're as close as I think we are, they might have spied us on their back trail." Yakima leveled a warning look at the dim-witted lawman.

"Oh," MacElvy said, narrowing one eye, sheepish. "Yeah . . ." Slowly, with an air of caution and keeping his gaze on the caprock, he pulled his hat down on his sweaty head.

"My feet are sore," Paloma said. "I am not walking anymore. I am riding. That's what the horse is for, no?" She led the steeldust over to a rock. She wasn't wearing the lawman's manacles now, as doing so would have slowed her up. MacElvy had only cuffed her and shackled her ankles at night—for good reason, as far as Yakima was concerned.

His head still ached from time to time.

MacElvy glanced at her. "Yeah, go ahead. It ain't so steep and rocky here, like before. Think I will, too."

Yakima shuttled his anxious gaze up the slope again. He thought it would be best if they stayed as low as possible, and a few seconds later he wanted to kick himself for not saying so. Because only a second after he had the thought, a bullet screeched through the air to his left.

A half-second after that, MacElvy's horse gave a fierce whinny, and a rifle's flat report echoed down from the knobs.

MacElvy was caught half in and half out of his saddle. He did not have a good grip on the horn or on the reins. When the big brown curveted and rose high on its hind legs, scissoring its front hooves toward the azure sky, MacElvy went flying with a shrill scream.

Yakima lost sight of him, his view blocked by the massive, pirouetting horse, but he heard the man give a yelp following a dull thud, as though his head had hit a rock.

"Shit!" Yakima said, glancing at Paloma. "Get down! Get down!"

Those last two words were drowned by the belches of two more rifles and the sharp smacks of bullets against rock or thudding into the ground and spewing gravel. Yakima quickly shucked his Winchester from his saddle scabbard and then laid the rifle sharply down against Wolf's ass, shouting, "Get out of here, boy! Go!"

Wolf needed little urging. As more rifles hammered away near the knob, sending lead sizzling down the slope and smashing into brush or rock or snapping branches of low, gnarled pines, the black neighed his disdain at the commotion, wheeled, and galloped back down the long slope in the direction from which they'd all come.

Paloma's horse was doing the same thing, but she hadn't dismounted fast enough. She lay in a heap near a wagon-sized boulder and a shrub oak, her dress pulled up around her waist. Her bare legs were curled beneath her.

She sat there frozen, staring at something on her left. For a second, Yakima thought she was addlepated, but then he saw the rattler coiled in the shade beside the boulder, not three feet away from the woman.

The viper was sticking its flat, diamond-shaped head out into the sunlight, its forked tongue testing the woman's scent. Its button tail was curled and quivering and beneath the continuing rifle fire, Yakima heard the spine-splintering whine of an imminent strike.

Crouching behind a boulder of his own, which the slugs hurled from above were hammering, Yakima raised the Yellowboy to his cheek, and fired.

The snake had just started to thrust its head and open jaws toward Paloma when the half-breed's bullet sliced it in two, about seven inches back from the head. The head still flew forward but landed in the dirt and gravel by the girl's bare right knee.

Paloma screamed and jerked backward, kicking at the snake's striking head. Bullets triggered from the knob plumed the dust around her, one striking the snake's head and turning it to dirty jelly. Yakima bounded out away from his boulder and, taking his rifle in his left hand, grabbed Paloma with his right. He jerked her to her feet and half-dragged her into some brush and mounded rocks.

He threw her down and turned to MacElvy. He cursed. The lawman lay in a small open area, head still propped against the low slab of rock he'd smashed it against. He lay on his back, arms and legs thrown wide. His eyes were closed. He was out like a blown lamp, but the slight rising and falling of his chest meant he wasn't dead.

Yet.

The bullets chewing into the sand and gravel around

him weren't a good indication he'd still be alive in the next several seconds. He was so out in the open, the bushwhackers could use him for target practice though it appeared they might have thought he was no longer worth wasting lead on. Most of the shots were now directed at the snag that Yakima and Paloma were in, the bullets spanging off rocks and snapping branches.

Keeping his head down, Yakima turned to the woman. "Can you shoot a rifle?"

She turned toward him, strands of hair pasted to her fear-flushed cheeks. "Of course."

Yakima cocked the Yellowboy and handed it to her. "Keep your head down, but try to send a few rounds up toward the knob. Don't worry about aiming; just throw some lead back at 'em, give me time to haul MacElvy's worthless carcass in here."

Paloma took the rifle in her hands, ran a hand erotically down the barrel, offering a crooked grin. "How do you know I won't shoot you with it?"

"I wish you would." Crouching, he turned toward MacElvy and said to Paloma, "Start shootin'!"

As Paloma snaked the Yellowboy's barrel over the top of the natural barricade, and started shooting, Yakima dashed out into the open, grabbed one of MacElvy's feet, and pulled. Two bullets kicked up gravel just behind him.

"Keep firing!" he shouted at Paloma.

"I'm doing all I can do, you bastard!" was the woman's sharp retort as she ejected a spent cartridge and pumped another one into the action.

"Now, no need for name-callin'," Yakima gritted out as he dragged the big lawman into the makeshift bunker.

"All right," Yakima told Paloma.

As she swung toward him a little too quickly for his taste, he grabbed the rifle out of her hands, and off-cocked the hammer. "Thanks."

She grinned through the dirt on her beautiful face, sliding a lock of hair back from her cheek with one hand. "Any time." She frowned, pouting. "Now, how in the hell are we going to get out of this? You've led us right into their trap!"

Ignoring her, Yakima dropped to a knee beside MacElvy. The man was breathing, but he was full out. Yakima reached a hand around to the back of the lawman's head, felt the blood from a gash.

The half-breed sighed, grumbled, "You stupid son of a . . . .." He saw no point in wasting his breath. The man was deep out and about as much use as the woman.

"Answer me!" Paloma said tautly.

Yakima whipped his head to her, pointed a gloved finger at her. "One more word out of you, I'm gonna beat you blue with a short stick."

She opened her mouth to retort, but snapped it shut.

She glared at him, and then sat back against a rock, drawing her raised knees toward her belly and crossing her arms over her breasts.

The ambushers continued their fusillade, their lead spanging off the rocks along the top of the natural barricade, a few hammering the boulder and the bole of a large oak on the other side of it.

Yakima shucked MacElvy's Remington from the lawman's holster and thrust it at Paloma. "Take this and use it if you have to."

"What are you going to do?"

"The only thing I can do under the circumstances."

"Which is what?"

"I'm gonna go up there and kill all your friends."

She studied him as he pulled the Yellowboy's loading tube out from beneath the octagonal barrel, and began punching fresh cartridges from one of his shell belts down the slide. She sidled over to him, placed a warm hand on his thigh.

"Yakima," she said. "If you find the money, don't forget about the other night. There can be plenty more where that one came from, amigo." She canted her head slightly, smiled sweetly, her dark eyes flashing.

Yakima rammed the loading tube home and locked it. "The only thing I remember about the other night is one hell of a head ache. Now keep your goddamn head down."

He turned away, began crawling toward the far end of the barricade. He paused and glanced over his shoulder at her. "Or don't. I don't care what you do!"

Then he rose, crouching, glanced over the barricade toward the knob against which smoke puffed from rifle barrels, and bounded off his heels.

"Darling, don't say that!" Paloma cried behind him, her voice all but drowned by the reinvigorated rifle fire.

Yakima ran a zigzagging course across a twenty-yard stretch of open ground. He vaulted a low hummock of sandy turf and hunkered down behind a flat-topped boulder roughly the size of a Denver hansom cab while the men from above blasted away at it. When the shooting dwindled, he bounded out from behind it and ran straight up the slope between shelving escarpments.

The shooters opened up again, lead spanging shrilly off the scarps, splattering Yakima's hat with pebbles and stone shards. There was good cover most of the way up the slope. They could shoot all they wanted. Let them use up their cartridges. What he wanted to do was start bringing them, one by one, into efficient shooting range of his Yellowboy.

There were five of them. Long odds, but he'd seen longer.

Yakima stopped and dropped to his butt, leaned back against a stone wall. He stared up the slope. The knob was turning apricot. Craning his head to look west, he saw that the sun was starting its drop behind the western ridges.

Dark soon. That was all right. The darker the better. He had good night vision. Besides, he was the hunter now. Jorgenson and the other outlaws were his quarry. Of course, that could change at any time, if they located him and surrounded him, but right now he held the better hand. The dark was better for the hunter than his prey.

Staying low behind boulders and jutting dykes and tufts of pines and cactus, he moved to his right along the shoulder of the slope. There was only sporadic shooting now as Jorgenson's men tried to draw his fire. They'd lost his position and were trying to relocate him. He was only about seventy yards or so from the knob at the crest of the slope, so it was time to slow down and be patient.

Patiently, he'd disorient them and take them down one at a time, the way he'd often taken down Apaches in the canyon lands farther north, back when he was a scout at Fort Hell. He'd learned the Apache way of fighting and used it against them. He'd use that tactic here.

Moving slowly, often crawling, he worked his way up the slope through the stone formations, letting the terrain itself be his guide. A couple of the outlaws were shouting back and forth but the breeze had come up and he couldn't hear what they were saying. Judging by the tones of their voices, he had them both puzzled and worried.

Suddenly, he stopped, dropped down behind a small, cracked boulder, and quickly doffed his hat.

Ahead and above him, about forty yards up the steep slope, a man in a black sombrero was moving toward him, striding cautiously between two large boulders turning the color of old pennies now as the sun continued to sink. The man was moving down a steep part of the slope between the boulders, holding his carbine in one hand, running his other, gloved hand along the boulder to his left for support.

Occasionally, Yakima could hear his spurs jingle faintly.

His face was round, eyes protruding from their sockets. His mouth was capped with a thick, black mustache. The ends of his mustache and his lime-green neckerchief ruffled in the breeze that was moaning amongst the rocks now and lifting occasional screens of tan dust.

Yakima raised his Yellowboy to his cheek, hoping that the fading rays of the sunlight angling over him from the west wouldn't glint off the barrel. But they must have. His quarry stopped suddenly and jerked his head up. He began to take his carbine in both hands.

Yakima squeezed the Yellowboy's trigger. As he did, one of his quarry's boots slipped on the steep slope and he lurched slightly to one side and fell to his butt. He screamed, dropping his carbine and clutching at the right side of his neck.

"He's here!" the Mexican shouted in English. "Here!"

Yakima pumped a fresh cartridge into the Yellowboy's breech. The Mexican turned onto his belly, pushed to his hands and knees, and began half-crawling, half-running up the slope between the boulders, spurs chiming raucously. He loosed red sand and gravel down the slope behind him.

Yakima fired the Yellowboy again, evoking another scream from the Mexican who grabbed the back of his right thigh. He screamed again. As Yakima fired again, the Mexican dragged himself to the mouth of the little canyon he was in, and darted behind the right boulder, falling.

Yakima's slug hammered a divot of stone from the side of the boulder where the Mexican's head had been a quarter-second before, the screech resounding off the face of the knob.

The bandit was out of sight, shouting in Spanish now, telling the others he was badly hit. He needed help.

Yakima doffed his hat, retreated thirty yards back down the slope, turned to his right, and ran in the opposite direction as before across the shoulder of the slope. He dropped down behind a low hummock of gravelly ground tufted with prickly pear and a lone cedar, and pressed his chest and belly flat. He removed his hat and held it flat against the ground, as well.

Pricking his ears to listen above his heart's drumming in his ears, he could hear the other bandits shouting to each other anxiously. At the same time, the man Yakima had wounded was screaming and begging for help in Spanish. He was losing a lot of blood, he was saying. He cursed them and continued to beg for help.

His screams dwindled, became sporadic.

The breeze picked up and moaned.

Gradually, the light faded across the broken slope, and the knob at the top of it became silhouetted against a darkening sky. When the orange ball of the sun had disappeared behind the toothy, black, western ridges, Yakima rose, doffed his hat, and began to make his way up the slope again, where the riflemen had fallen ominously silent.

The whining and moaning of the breeze sounded like a stalking mountain lion.

Had the bandits abandoned the knob, fallen back in retreat despite the fact they were being hunted by only one man?

Yakima received his answer a minute later. As he continued to crawl, sniffing the breeze like a coyote or an Apache, he scented the sour sweat and leather smell of a man . . .

20

In the darkness behind the natural stone barricade, Paloma crouched, listening, waiting.

Up the slope, a rifle cracked.

The rifle cracked again and there was one more report so close on its heels that it had to have come from another gun.

Silence rained down like lead from the direction of the knob. A new moon was rising, turning the sky behind the knob a dark purple. In the moon's wan light, the knob itself shouldered, the brown of old cowhide, against the dim stars.

The silence grew heavier as Paloma waited for more gunfire. Or, perhaps, there wouldn't be anymore. Maybe Yakima had finished Jorgenson's bunch, as he'd promise. Or maybe Jorgenson's bunch had killed Yakima.

Her heart thudding tensely in her ears, wondering

about the money, Paloma waited.

Her palms resting against her thighs were clammy. To her left, MacElvy groaned. The lawman moved his head slightly. In the faint, pearl light being shed by the thumbnail moon rising in the east, she could see the lawman's pale eyelids flutter. He groaned again, drew a deep breath, exhaled, and lay still.

Paloma turned toward the top of the barricade and the brown knob rising beyond it. Was the fight over? If so, who had won? Where were the saddlebags bulging with her money? That's how she saw the money now—as hers. Not stolen payroll loot but as money that belonged to her and that had been stolen from her.

She was almost relieved when a man shouted from the direction of the knob, and more rifles cracked. She lifted her head to see over the barricade, and saw an orange flash followed by the rocketing report of the rifle. She saw another flash a little left of the first one. More rifles spoke though she couldn't see the flashes of those.

The fight was still on. Yakima was still alive. That meant that the fate of the saddlebags had not yet been decided.

Paloma swallowed, blinked, ran her bare arm across her sweat-moist forehead. Since their fate had not yet been decided, why shouldn't she herself decide it while the men were busy shooting each other?

Her heart hammered so anxiously, hopefully at the thought that she thought it would crack her breastbone.

Biting down on her lower lip, she picked up MacElvy's pistol. She cast another look up toward the knob. A breeze had risen, moaning and rustling, and beneath it she could hear a man yelling somewhere up there in the darkness. Quickly, she slipped out of her blood shoes. Barefoot, she'd be quieter, and it would be easier for her to climb the gravelly slope.

Holding the pistol in both hands, she rose to a crouch and cautiously stole out from behind the barricade. Her skin prickled with the anticipation of bullets being hurled at her, but she suppressed the anxiety and forced herself to move slowly, deliberately up the slope.

She angled left as she climbed the mountain, intending to skirt the area where she'd seen the rifle flashes. If she could make her way to the knob and discover Jorgenson's camp, she'd also find the saddlebags. Since he and his men were hunting Yakima, they'd probably left the saddlebags in their camp. Near their horses. If she lay her hands on both the saddlebags and a horse . . .

The anticipation caused her body to shudder, and her heart to hiccup. Inadvertently, she increased her pace and caught herself, set one bare foot deliberately down in front of the other.

"Slowly," she whispered. "Slowly, slowly . . ."

Suddenly, she stopped and wheeled to peer behind her. She'd thought she heard the crunch of gravel under a furtive foot.

She gasped, raised the pistol in both hands, expecting to see someone running toward her from the downslope. There was nothing behind her except an upthrust thumb of tortured rock and a cedar to its left.

She dropped to a knee, trying to hold the heavy pistol out in front of her. Another sound, the same as before, to her right. She gasped and swung the pistol in that direction.

Still, nothing.

The moon was stretching eerie shadows but none seemed to be moving. The rocks and boulders were brown in the pearl-limned darkness, the brush and cactus purple.

The breeze lifted dust in front of her. The fine particles peppered her eyes, caused her to blink.

"Who's there?" she whispered. "Yakima?" She paused. "MacElvy, is that you?"

Up the slope, a rifle thundered. As she gave another startled gasp and turned in that direction, more rifles crackled, slugs spanging shrilly.

A shadow moved to her right, glowing long and angling up the slope in front of her from behind. Before she could wheel again, arms were wrapped around her and one gloved hand closed tightly over her mouth while the other slashed forward to jerk the pistol from her hand. The glove was over her nose as well as her mouth, tasting and smelling like smoky buckskin, cutting off her wind.

She tried to fight, but the man was tall and strong and he had her in what felt like a death grip. He leaned back. She heard him grunt softly. Her bare feet came off the ground and she was dangling in mid-air, her toes several inches above the slope. She tried to kick and flail her arms but his hand over her mouth and nose instantly fatigued her, thrust her quickly toward unconsciousness.

A voice said into her right ear in Spanish, "Dearest Paloma, I will set you down and remove my hand from your mouth if you promise to not make a sound." The voice was eerily familiar. So familiar, in fact, that she shuddered at the sound of it. His smell was familiar, was well.

The man squeezed her harder, shaking her. "Do you promise?"

Quickly, her lungs constricting and her heart banging loudly at the lack of oxygen, she nodded.

He set her down. He removed his hand from her mouth.

Paloma continued to stare up the slope, seeing nothing, shuddering. She felt the man behind her. She did not want to turn around.

PETER BRANDVOLD

Finally, she turned her head to gaze back over her shoulder.

The face beneath the sombrero was the same one she'd seen through the balcony door at Ballantrae's saloon. Though one eye was eggshell white in the moonlight, and little black sores pocked his face, the face belonged to none other than Octavio La Paz.

He smiled, slitting his one good eye, the one the Apaches hadn't ruined with the end of a burning stick.

Paloma felt as though a black cloth had been thrown over the world.

Suddenly her knees were buckling and everything was quickly going dark.

***

Water splashed on her face. It was like a cold slap, and instantly she was awake, lifting her head from a hard stone floor and blinking the water out of her eyes.

"Oh, my god!" she cried, staring into the face again of Octavio La Paz now lit by the shunting light and shadows of small, orange flames. "It is you. But it can't be you. For the love of all the saints in Heaven, Octavio, I killed you!"

She wanted to flee but she was hogtied, wrists tied to her ankles behind her, and lying on her side, one strap of her dress dangling to the stone floor.

228

"Keep your voice down," he said, scowling over his shoulder at the opening of what apparently was a cave they were in. "You want to wake the dead?" He turned back to her, chuckling. There was an insane look in his good eye.

She just stared at him, not quite sure she could believe she was actually staring at Octavio La Paz. Waves of terror rippled through her.

He smiled, touched the oozing ulcers on his cheeks. "Ahh . . . you wonder why I'm not dead. I came close. But fortunately my brother had an antidote to snakeroot. And old Apache remedy. The same one they used to cure the clap. A tincture of rattlesnake venom, a paste of crow's liver, and various herbs including shagbark brewed into a foul-smelling tea. It's not supposed to work without an Apache witch blessing it after hanging a coyote skull over a bowl of the stuff for twenty-four hours, during a full moon. Such a witch gave it to my brother as an offering, when she acquired religion. Apparently, it's rather common around Horsetooth for wives to poison their husbands in such a way. Evil bitches!"

La Paz chuckled.

He touched an ulcer just above his blind white eye, beneath the bandanna he wore over his hairless scalp. "Just what the doctor ordered, as they say. Still, your toxic poison fried my guts and caused these eruptions on my face. I may never be a man again," he snarled, taking her face in his hand and pinching her mouth into a small 'O'." But at least I will have the satisfaction of having run you down, you little *puta* bitch."

He released her face and sat back on his rear, drawing his knees up and wrapping his arms around them.

The fire played across his skull-like, once-handsome face with its oozing ulcers and hollow jaws. "I'd stopped convulsing by the next morning. My anger fueled the healing, you see. I felt on top of the world by noon . . . despite a little weakness and nausea . . . so I saddled a fast horse and led another fast horse behind me, so I could switch off and catch up to you all the faster. Tracked you down, followed you and your friends from a distance, biding my time. I was still a little weak, and, blinded in one eye, I decided to wait until I could get you alone . . . and get close enough to do the killing most *efficiently*. Now, here we are at last."

"I don't understand," Paloma said, looking around at the small cavern and the crackling fire. Tack was strewn everywhere—saddles, blankets, bridles, saddlebags, cooking utensils. Outside, occasional rifle shots told her the battle for the money—*her* money—was still being waged on the slope below the knob. "Where are we?"

"This is Jorgenson's camp."

Paloma's jaw hinges loosened as she stared at La Paz's ghostly, silhouetted visage in shock.

"I came upon it just after the shooting started. Jorgenson and his men were distracted, so I thought I'd loot their lair here for the money. My money. Don't worry—it's not here," he said, when Paloma began casting her wide-eyed gaze around. "I went through all the gear. Jorgenson probably has the saddlebags with him. He, too, sniffed out your trail about half a day before you reached the saloon.

"As for me, I would have caught up to you, but I got waylaid by Apaches, same as your half-breed friend and the lawman, but I managed to run their gauntlet with far fewer injuries than before. I guess I learned from pervious miseries. My friend Jorgenson must have been scouring the mountains for me when he saw you, recognized the pretty Mexican flower riding alone, and followed you to Ballantrae's saloon. Tell me, Chiquita, how did he manage to get his hands on the money?"

Paloma sighed and stared at the floor, crestfallen. "Let's just say I was foolish."

"Oh, we can say that, all right. You were foolish from the start, my flower. It is well known by the old people that it's bad luck to poison a man. Especially one who loves you . . . as I did."

His gaze was fleetingly pensive, his good eye turning soft. Just as quickly it hardened, and his cheeks dimpled over his jaw joints. "And now, as soon as those men are done killing each other out there, and I have the money once again, I'm going to kill you slow."

He jerked a knife up from somewhere on his person and held it up over the fire, the light flashing off the long, wide blade. He laid the flat of the blade against the back of her naked right thigh—she gasped at the chill—and slid it slowly up to her exposed right buttock. "I'm going to savor every second of it."

He angled the point down between her thighs.

21

Yakima hunkered Indian style in a cleft beneath a cab-in-sized boulder, the right rear corner of which angled sharply back upon itself. The ground also sloped sharply back toward the corner of the rock. In this depression Yakima sat, as he'd been sitting for most of the night, waiting and listening.

He stared almost straight east. The eastern horizon had turned light green and salmon above a long, straight line of smoky white.

Dawn.

The moon had long since set.

Birds were chirping in the brush around him, flitting here and there, their wings flashing silver. A kangaroo sat a few feet away from him, in the purple shadow of another boulder, watching the half-breed suspiciously as it munched on the grass stem he held between his two front paws.

Suddenly, the rat dropped the grass and scuttled back behind the boulder, giving a little indignant screech and disappearing.

Yakima's back tightened.

He closed his hands around his Yellowboy's stock. Something had spooked the rat.

He'd killed three of the five outlaws so far, their bodies strewn a good distance apart across the slope. He wasn't sure the other two were still around but he'd decided to wait till daylight to find out. Many a scout had saddled a cloud because he hadn't been as patient as an Apache.

So, he waited, ears pricked, hands slowly tightening around the breech and stock of the Yellowboy he held across the buckles of his shell belts. Several minutes later, he heard what the rat must have heard, the very quiet crackle of boots on gravel.

His heart quickened. The other two outlaws were still here. He was glad. He'd have hated to be wasting his time out here and to still have to track the last two even deeper into Mexico. He'd come this far, he wasn't giving up on retrieving the money for the bounty that MacElvy had promised.

If the lawman was still alive that was. Or if his unceremonious meeting with that rock hadn't turned him into a blubbering idiot. Anyway, Yakima was getting the money back one way or another. He'd been through too much to let it go now.

Breathing slowly, calmly through his mouth, he waited.

Gradually, the soft crunch of boots on gravel grew louder.

Then one of those boots appeared in Yakima's field of vision. It was a badly scuffed, brown leather boot almost white with scuffmarks and dust, and soft as a moccasin. It had a high, undershot, Mexican-style heel. It bore the dark strap marks of a spur, which had wisely been removed so the jingle wouldn't give its wearer away.

The heel of the boot lifted and then the other boot appeared slightly ahead of the first one as well as a good six inches of a deerskin legging. This second, left boot was nearly identical to the right one--right down to the strap marks from the missing spur.

Both boots remained frozen in place for nearly a minute. Then the right boot moved slowly ahead of the left one as their owner moved from Yakima's left to his right, down the incline that was less steep here than elsewhere.

The left boot came slowly, gingerly down, followed by the right and then the left one again.

Yakima turned his rifle butt-out and slammed the butt as hard as he could against the left boot. There was a clipped shriek as both feet were rammed out from beneath the man wearing the boots, and a sharp smack sounded as the boot-owner's head struck the side of the boulder beneath which Yakima sat. The man dropped his rifle and fell on the ground—writhing and clutching at his left ankle.

Yakima hustled out from his hiding place and stood over the short, skinny Mexican, and frowned. The whole left side of the man's face looked like old rotting hamburger. It was swollen and pocked with little holes, and that ear was entirely gone. Not just shredded like MacElvy's ear, but entirely gone. In its place was what looked like semi-dry cherry jam.

The little Mexican looked up at Yakima, and stopped writhing. He looked so badly abused that Yakima hesitated to abuse him further.

He shouldn't have hesitated. A voice in his head told him so a half-second before a man's voice outside of his head—behind him, in fact—also admonished him with: "Stop, big man, or I'll drill you right between the shoulders!"

Yakima swung around to see a tall American with a long, horsey face sheathed in pewter sideburns and dressed in gaudy Mexican garb holding a Winchester carbine on him, lifting his mouth corners in a delighted grin. He wore a large black and red sombrero, the thong drawn taut against his chin.

Saddlebags were draped over his left shoulder. Not

just any saddlebags, but *the* saddlebags bulging with the Army payroll loot. They were hard not to recognize.

"Drop the Yellowboy," the American said in a menacingly affable voice.

Yakima crouched and set the Yellowboy down on the ground by his right boot.

"Kick it away."

Yakima kicked it away. Then the American told him to shuck his Colt with two fingers of his left hand, and toss that way, as well. Yakima didn't see that he had much choice. The American had him dead to rights from six feet away. He was most likely going to die but he saw no reason to rush a likely awkward encounter with St. Peter.

He tossed away the Colt.

"Miguel, stop moaning like a whipped dog and get up!" the American scolded the little Mexican.

Miguel did as he was told. Limping on his bad ankle and giving Yakima the hairy eyeball, he picked up his own rifle and strode daintily back to stand beside the tall American in the fancily stitched garb of a Mexican vaquero.

Yakima said, "Jorgenson?"

"That's right. You?"

"Yakima Henry."

The morning light grew, reflected in Jorgenson's pale blue eyes beneath the broad brim of his fancy sombrero, as those eyes raked Yakima up and down. "Half-breed."

Yakima didn't say anything.

"I've heard the name. You carry a reputation, Henry." Jorgenson rolled his eyes around as though to take in the entire slope on which they'd all spent the night exchanging lead. "I see why."

"Shoot him," said little Miguel, standing daintily on his no-doubt broken ankle, stretching his lips back from his large, white teeth as he snarled up at Yakima, who towered over him. "Shoot him now! Why all the talk?"

"Don't be so hasty, Miguel. This man did us a favor."

Miguel scowled incredulously up at the tall American. "What favor?"

"He whittled our herd down considerably." Jorgenson smiled down at the saddlebags. "That makes more for us. Or . . . more for me, I should say."

Miguel frowned. Keeping his smiling eyes on Yakima, Jorgenson swung his rifle across his belly toward Miguel.

Miguel had just opened his mouth to yell, when Jorgenson's rifle spoke. Miguel stumbled backward, dropping his rifle and clutching his belly with both hands. He fell and lay writhing, drawing both knees to his ruined middle, gasping through gritted teeth. Jorgenson put him out of his misery with a bullet to his left temple.

Yakima lunged for Jorgenson but the American was ready for that. He quickly jerked his rifle back toward the half-breed, stepping slowly backward, that maddeningly affable smile on his face.

"Make a deal with ya," Jorgenson said.

"Oh, yeah?"

"You throw in with me, I'll give you a third."

Yakima scowled at him, curious.

Jorgenson shrugged. "A man needs a partner. Me? I'm fresh out."

"That's what greed will do to a man," Yakima opined. "And you wouldn't be able to trust me anymore than you trusted them"—he glanced at little Miguel—"or they trusted you."

A rifle belched somewhere behind Jorgenson.

The American's eyes snapped wide and he lurched sideways with a gasp. He swung heavily around, his rifle sagging in his arms, and then another shot rang out.

Jorgenson stumbled backward across little Miguel and fell to his butt, cursing like a gut-shot coyote, clamping both hands over the hole in his upper left chest from which frothy blood spurted.

Another man appeared on the slope above him. A Mexican in black leather leggings and with a red bandanna showing beneath the brim of his green, steeple-crowned sombrero. He wore a green sash above his pistol belt, and a long, black leather duster hung to the heels of his silver-tipped, black boots. He laughed as he moved down the slope, holding his rifle butt against his hip, aiming the barrel at Yakima. As he drew near, Yakima saw the sores on his face, and the one blind eye.

"Welcome to the party!" Yakima said, beckoning to the man with exaggerated vehemence. "The more the merrier!"

"Gracias, amigo," the newcomer said. "I don't mind if I do. Kindly keep away from your weapons or I will kill you now rather than later." He stood over the writhing form of Jorgenson, who glared up at him, his sombrero smashed flat against the ground behind him. "You devil! I thought she killed you!"

Yakima scowled at the newcomer with the diseased-looking face, and then he laughed. "Well, I'll be damned," he said in exasperation. "Here we've all be blamin' the innocent Miss Paloma for your demise, La Paz. But she didn't kill you at all, did she?"

Yakima laughed insanely. He truly thought he was going insane. Everything just seemed funny to him now. Like it was all such a big, insanely funny joke that he didn't even really mind that a big part of it was on him.

Including when Jorgenson glared up at Octavio La Paz and said, "A devil is what you are, La Paz. A double-crossing devil!"

"Don't call me that," La Paz said, glowering, his pale cheeks reddening with anger. "I don't like to be called a devil. It casts doubt on a man's character and brings bad luck to his family!"

He calmly drilled a rifle round through Jorgenson's forehead. Jorgenson's legs twitched across the slumped body of little Miguel and then the American outlaw rolled onto his side, and died.

Keeping his rifle aimed at Yakima, Octavio La Paz walked over to Jorgenson and crouched to pick up the saddlebags, which he brushed off and draped over his left shoulder.

"Now," he said to Yakima. "What to do about you . . ."

As if in reply to his question, another rifle blasted.

It blew La Paz's sombrero off his head, revealing the red, blood stained bandanna stretched across the top of his scalped head. La Paz screamed and wheeled to his left, and the rifle barked twice more. Both slugs slammed into the outlaw's chest, throwing him straight backwards off little Miguel and Jorgenson.

He shook a boot once, gave a long, ragged sigh, blinking his good eye, and then lay still.

Behind the boulder on Yakima's left, hooves clomped. The sun was up now, and it shone salmon on the dust that rose as the brown horse came into view along the base of the copper-colored knob. MacElvy rode lazily in the saddle, extending his rifle out one-handed, aiming the barrel at the three bodies clumped to Yakima's right.

"Good morning," the lawman said, grinning and swinging heavily down from his saddle.

He moved down the slope, kicking up dust with every heavy step. He looked pale and haggard, his face and ear the same mess as before, but otherwise no worse for the wear. He still wore the bandanna like a patch across his cut eye.

"Damn," Yakima said, unable to keep from loosing a few more bars of skeptical laughter. "I didn't think I'd ever say this, MacElvy, but I sure am glad to see you."

The half-breed moved to retrieve his rifle.

"Not so fast, Yakima."

22

Yakima stopped, looked at MacElvy. The lawman had his Winchester aimed at Yakima's belly. MacElvy's eyes were hard and cold.

Yakima chuckled giddily. "You ain't a lawman at all, are you?"

"Of course I am. The girl was lyin' through her pretty teeth, as usual. Just now, though, I decided to quit." MacElvy walked over to the pile of bloody dead men. Keeping his rifle trained on Yakima, he crouched and picked up the saddlebags. "I been through too damn much to give this loot up now."

Yakima chuckled.

MacElvy draped the saddlebags over his shoulder. "What's so funny?"

"You are. All of it is."

"All of what?"

"All of this, you damn fool."

MacElvy's broad face reddened. "You ain't gonna be thinkin' it's so funny after I kill you."

Yakima laughed again. "You ain't gonna kill me."

"Oh, no?" It was the outlaw lawman's turn to laugh. "Why not?"

"Because she's gonna kill you first!"

MacElvy's eyes widened. He stared blankly past Yakima. The outlaw turned slowly, tensely around in time to see Paloma just before she shot him.

The woman strode down the slope from the base of the knob. She was holding a pistol in both hands—MacElvy's own Remington. Smoke licked up out of the barrel. Her long, black hair blew around her pretty head in the rising, hot, dry, morning wind.

Dust lifted around her bare feet and the leg exposed by the long tear in her skirt. One strap of the dress dangled down her arm. The filthy dress looked as though it was about to fall right off her voluptuous figure.

She said nothing but only kept her cool, dark eyes as well as the cocked Remington's barrel on Yakima. She crouched and picked up the blood-splattered saddlebags, slung them over her shoulder.

She regarded Yakima blankly for a time, and then canted her head to one side and arched her left brow. "Join me?"

Yakima looked at the cocked gun in her hand.

"We could have a good time together," she said. "This is a lot of money. We could go into business together."

"The confidence game business?"

"Why not? I'm good at it. I've had a lot of practice over the years. A girl needs some way of making a living, and I never was much into doing it on my back."

"Sure had me fooled."

She hardened her voice with frustration and urgency. "Join me!"

"Nah. I don't think so, Paloma."

She pursed her lips, nodded slowly, regretfully. Yakima watched the pistol in her hands, felt his belly tighten in anticipation of the bullet. She held the gun on him for close to another minute, and then she raised the barrel and depressed the hammer.

Yakima loosed a slow, relieved breath.

"Good-bye, Yakima," she said, backing away up the slope, toward where MacElvy's horse stood, watching them both warily.

He pinched his hat brim to her.

She continued on up the slope. She grabbed the brown's reins, slung the saddlebags over her back, and climbed into the saddle.

She tossed her head at Yakima, and rode off along the base of the knob, heading east and then most likely south

PETER BRANDVOLD

toward the Gulf of California. She stopped the horse suddenly, and smiled over her shoulder at the half-breed. "You know what?"

"No, I don't know much of anything."

"Well, I know something. I know that we will meet up again someday, my big, handsome half-breed friend. And I think we will have more fun than before."

Yakima watched her put the horse into a rocking-chair canter and dwindle to a brown blur pulling a soft, tan dust cloud along the base of the knob.

He sighed and said, "I sure hope not."

Then he gathered his weapons and headed on down the mountain in search of his horse and a trail. Any trail. To anywhere.

It didn't much matter.

A Look At: Bloody Arizona:
A Yakima Henry Western

ONE HELL OF A BLOOD-SPLASHED, ROUGH
WESTERN TALE.

Yakima Henry is holed up in an old prospector's cabin
in the wilds of south-central Arizona, between Tucson
and Lordsburg, New Mexico. He's decided to cool his
heels until fall, prospecting for gold and hoping for a little
color with which to fund a trek into Mexico.

The half-breed wanderer just can't shake Faith's memory, however. Not even with the help of the firewater
and pretty whore in the Busted Flush Saloon in the little
nowhere town of Apache Springs. The firewater causes
the crazed, jade-eyed half-breed to go into a rage and
bust up the saloon and half the men in the town until he's
finally subdued and carted over to the local jail – locked
up by his friend, Town Marshal Lon Taggart.

AVAILABLE OCTOBER 2021

ABOUT THE AUTHOR

Peter Brandvold grew up in the great state of North Dakota in the 1960's and '70s, when television westerns were as popular as shows about hoarders and shark tanks are now, and western paperbacks were as popular as Game of Thrones.

Brandvold watched every western series on television at the time. He grew up riding horses and herding cows on the farms of his grandfather and many friends who owned livestock.

Brandvold's imagination has always lived and will always live in the West. He is the author of over a hundred lightning-fast action westerns under his own name and his pen name, Frank Leslie.